TEN YEARS! IT'S H... years ago I sent off my first manuscript—and all my hopes—to LOVESWEPT. I had never dared to submit before, but I had watched as this new line began to change the romance industry.

LOVESWEPT was doing things no other publisher had even thought to do. It took chances with exciting story lines and untried authors. It was the first to bring romance writers out of the closet, introducing real writers with real names and real lives to its readers. And it took a chance on me.

So now we celebrate our anniversaries together. Congratulations and here's to our next ten!

WHAT ARE *LOVESWEPT* ROMANCES?

They are stories of true romance and touching emotion. We believe those two very important ingredients are constants in our highly sensual and very believable stories in the LOVESWEPT line. Our goal is to give you, the reader, stories of consistently high quality that may sometimes make you laugh, sometimes make you cry, but are always fresh and creative and contain many delightful surprises within their pages.

Most romance fans read an enormous number of books. Those they truly love, they keep. Others may be traded with friends and soon forgotten. We hope that each LOVESWEPT romance will be a treasure—a "keeper." We will always try to publish

LOVE STORIES YOU'LL NEVER FORGET
BY AUTHORS YOU'LL ALWAYS REMEMBER

The Editors

Loveswept® 623

THE DOCTOR TAKES A WIFE

KIMBERLI WAGNER

BANTAM BOOKS
NEW YORK • TORONTO • LONDON • SYDNEY • AUCKLAND

THE DOCTOR TAKES A WIFE
A Bantam Book / June 1993

*If you would be interested in receiving protective vinyl
covers for your Loveswept books, please write to this
address for information:*

*Loveswept
Bantam Books
P.O. Box 985
Hicksville, NY 11802*

ISBN 0-553-44284-8

Published simultaneously in the United States and Canada

PRINTED IN THE UNITED STATES OF AMERICA

OPM   0 9 8 7 6 5 4 3 2 1

Special thanks to:

Officer Kent Van der Kamp, LAPD

Santa Anita Racetrack
The Office of the Horse Identifier
Diane Piper
Sandy King
and Candace
for being so generous with your time,
tours, and answers to 1001 questions

Christine Davenport, Jockey
all my admiration for your
courage, skill, and determination

Rick Kessler, Thoroughbred Breeder

Angelo Bonnadonna

Mike Lessa
who made it fun

&

Janis Kristjanson
critic extraordinaire
and unfailing supporter

ONE

"Again, Muñiz?" Connor groused as he pushed the curtain back in a one-arm sweep. His patient sat on the edge of the bed, feet swinging idly. With the white curtain, white bed, she was the only thing of brightness.

Nurse Carlotta Muñiz grinned at the sight. Dr. Connor MacLeod shook his head and snapped the chart closed.

"What the de'il is it that ye do, girl," he demanded crisply, "to break these puir hands over and over this way?"

"You know what I do, Connor." Alixandra Benton answered him in a tolerant singsong. "I run wild beasties around a dirt track while guys with pencils behind their ears holler at me."

"Aye, so you've said." Connor scowled at her from beneath dark brows. "But according to your records, you spend more time here with me than you spend high on your thoroughbreds." He shook his head at the lass who might have been no more than sixteen years of age. Her dark blond fairy hair curled down her back in a crazy tangle, but it was her eyes, blue-green as the sea, that made a man look again.

Very American, she was. Her clothes were tight, faded blue jeans and a pink T-shirt that ended at her midriff. She was full of vinegar, this one, with ever an answer handy . . . even when she was in pain. And he'd seen her in pain a number of times.

He looked again at the chart that listed her age as twenty-four, though her size and bone structure gave that number the lie.

The scowl was back. "Who is with you today?"

"Doc," she answered, smiling sweetly, "it's my hand, not my head."

"This time."

Alix couldn't help the grin. She had liked this giant Scot from the first, the first time he'd taped her wrist the year before, when she'd been brought in from the track after a fall. He had the most gentle hands.

His frown had been so fierce, his concern so

intense. It had been comforting, somehow, to have a complete stranger care that much about her welfare, especially a man whose very occupation should make him callous to others' pain.

Her Dr. Connor was six two or three, with shoulders as wide as a beam beneath the white coat. She wasn't often around men so . . . large. But she liked the way she had to look up to see him, and the way his long dark lashes curled over his chocolate-colored eyes in contrast to his pale skin. He looked like a man with lots of children. She wondered if they had his eyes.

"If you want to give me a temporary," she said, "I'll come back to the clinic for my cast in a couple of days when the swelling's down."

"Oh, aye." He raised a dark brow at her with lazy sarcasm. "Now ye're a physician."

"Let's just say I'm experienced in the field." She grinned cockily.

"Might I ask, then, why there is so verra much swelling, Alixandra?" His fingers grazed over the bruised flesh.

"I didn't think it was broken," she answered. The truth was she hadn't wanted it to be broken.

"An' you a vet'ran," he said dryly, shocking Alix into staring up at him.

"Connor! Humor?"

"Ye're underweight," he announced.

"I'm an athlete."

"For you, you're underweight." Connor worked at giving her his worst bedside manner, for the feel of her skin was disturbing and he didn't like the distraction. "And a horse did this?"

"Mmm." She nodded. "He wheeled on me— the reins—Bad habit of Pride's. But it doesn't happen too often."

"To you it does—twice in sixteen months. A hammer would be quicker."

"Ah, but not nearly so much fun." She hid her grin, because she would hate it if she did anything to cause this caring man to lose face.

He flipped the chart closed and gave it to the nurse. "Och, well." He looked up and his eyes met hers with an intent message she couldn't read. "Let's get ye on yer way."

"Pretty tough, Doc." A small laugh escaped her, but he only glowered and reached again for the injured hand.

When he was finished, he left the cubicle with Nurse Muñiz hot on his heels. His thoughts were unprofessional, he scolded himself, and she was much too young for him. As they passed the desk, he rubbed his thumb against his forefinger thoughtfully and announced, "If that young woman is admitted to emergency again, it might be better if she sees someone else."

"Yes, Doctor." Head nurse Muñiz was rarely startled and never surprised, but at this her brows rose. Her interest too.

Later, Alix thought about her Dr. Connor as she walked to her car through an unexpected rainstorm. He had obviously gotten used to handling the small community's demands, as well as the racetrack traffic. But he still seemed out of place.

She guessed him to be in his late thirties, early forties. His face was strong and well lined. He didn't seem the kind of man who would be happy living in Southern California.

He hadn't lost his intensity or gained a tan in the time she had known him. She could more easily picture him in some rugged place where life was more difficult, with challenges of nature to be conquered each day, Wyoming maybe, or Alaska.

Smiling at her odd notions, Alix turned her mind to her problems with Pride of Place, the willful gelding she'd been riding. Opening the low door of her Alfa-Romeo, she stopped dead, staring inside. Oh, yeah. A stick shift.

Dumb. Very dumb.

Connor walked from the hospital, wearing a starched trench coat over his suit, a huge black umbrella bobbing above him.

The girl had parked in "Doctors Only" again, he noted, next to his Saab. It would be hard to miss the diminutive figure standing beside the open door of the little red car.

"Trouble, lass?" he asked casually.

Alix started and looked around, a friendly recognition in her eyes.

She shrugged. "Can't drive."

"How did you get here?" he asked, glancing over her. Her hair straggled down her back, shiny wet. The T-shirt was well-doused, and she didn't seem to notice. But she was a lovely thing, even in the rain.

"Well," she said resignedly, "I didn't have a brace then."

Connor stared at her in disbelief. American, with money enough for a sports car and a hillside address, and still she hadn't any idea how to take care of herself. Hurtling down a track on a beast three grown men couldn't manage in a tantrum, driving with a broken hand, standing there dripping and cold in the rain and no way home. A waif.

"Lock up and come along, then."

Alix watched him walk around his car and open the trunk, then close it and return to her with a big gray towel. He handed her his umbrella to hold above them. Then he draped the towel carefully across his leather upholstery.

Alix grinned to herself. She'd never known a man who carried towels in his trunk for the occasional spring shower. She wasn't even disturbed that he hadn't offered the towel to her before the upholstery.

When he straightened, though, he stripped off his raincoat and placed it over her shoulders. That stopped all thought entirely. The last time a man had made a gallant gesture in her direction, it had been a five-foot jockey who hadn't hit her with his "stick" during a race when she knew he was dying to do it.

Amazed, she looked up to find Connor wearing his habitual scowl.

"In," he commanded, towering over her.

She got in, then watched him as he slid into the driver's seat. He looked tired. Black stubble was beginning to show beneath his pale skin, and this close, she could see the circles beneath his eyes and the lines spanning from their corners.

"I appreciate this," she said. His only answer was a short grunt before he leaned across her to tug her seat belt into place.

He smelled of rain, and man, and very faintly of after-shave. Not expensive French cologne, but the kind of after-shave she remembered her grandfather had used.

He seemed to know where he was going before she gave him the address. "Your med file," he explained when he saw her surprise. "We share the same street. I've even seen you run by sometimes."

She had to stare at that.

To her amazement, he seemed embarrassed, ducking his head.

When he pulled into her drive, she turned to say thanks. She caught him with one hand squeezing the back of his neck as if he were trying to get a kink out.

She drew in a slow breath. "Would you like some coffee?"

He stared out the windshield and finally seemed to come to some kind of decision. "Aye," he sighed. "I would."

She tried to keep her surprise from showing. From the look on his face, she would have thought he was anxious to be rid of her.

Coffee. She hoped she had some.

She fumbled at the catch to her seat belt and felt his fingers cover hers, pressing the release. When she put her brace upon the door handle, trying to remember if she had picked up her clothes from the bedroom carpet, he made a tsking sound and reached across her to drag her arm back into her lap. Then he got out of the car and came around for her.

She must have seemed startled because his brows drew even closer together. But it gave her the strangest feeling, just to see him standing there, holding that big umbrella.

Alix stepped up to the high, weathered gray wood fence that bordered her front yard and pushed at the gate. Down four flagstone steps, then she fumbled awkwardly for her key until he took her purse from her. He plucked her keys out and fit the right one into the lock as a fierce, unladylike sneeze overtook her. The next thing she felt was the imprint of a great, warm hand in the center of her back.

"Go away in, lass."

Alix went in.

Because the house was surrounded by windows on all sides, the gloom from the rain had spilled into every room. Alix flipped the switches by the door, and warmth flooded with the light. She looked around self-consciously and tried to see her house as Connor might see it. She liked pine and natural tones; California cream, palest tan, and peach, all of them quiet, cool.

One quick glance showed her she had left a newspaper on the coffee table, but, thankfully, no clothes tossed over the furniture.

Smiling with new bravado, she gathered up the paper in hurried motions as she said, "Make yourself at home."

In the bedroom, she changed into a long turquoise sweater and pants. The wet clothes, she tossed in the closet. Not that he would be coming into her bedroom.

She dragged on wool socks, sighing with pleasure, then dried her hair until it turned to a fine mass of curls. When she padded through the living room to the kitchen, Connor was staring out at the San Gabriel Mountains.

When she returned from the kitchen with the coffee, she found him still at the wide windows, his back to her. He had taken off his suit jacket. It lay on a chair.

Alix blinked and finished carrying the coffee tray into the room. His body was thoroughbred all right; wide at the shoulders and chest, tapered waist leading to huge thighs. His rump was round with muscle. He rubbed once more at the back of his neck as he turned toward her.

"You're tired." She smiled gently, trying not to stare at those thighs.

"Double shift, and I've near forgotten what it feels like to sleep."

Alix wasn't surprised. The clinic physicians kept notoriously crazy hours and caught the overflow from the nearest hospital, which was ten miles farther away from the track. Most of the jocks preferred to be taken directly to the clinic. They were treated with less fuss in less time.

"Coffee is probably the last thing you need." She looked at his cup worriedly.

"Och, I'm immune." He smiled down at her, and her lips parted soundlessly. It was the first real smile she'd ever seen from him, a dazzling sight.

"Oh." She held her sigh back. "Uh, how do you take it?"

Sitting on the couch, he stared at her as he reached for a cup. "Just so."

Alix sat on the ottoman near the coffee table and pushed the plate of apples, cheese, pâté, and crackers toward him.

"Mmm, food," he murmured before he attacked the plate. He seemed pleased by the sight. Amazed, Alix watched him finish half the plate before she muttered something about being right back, and ran to the kitchen for more.

"Turkey, there should be some turkey in here," she muttered, rummaging one-handed in the fridge. She slapped together a gigantic sandwich and dashed back into the living room. Her big Scot was looking shamefaced. The plate on the coffee table was clean except for a bare grape stem.

"I'm sorry, lass. Canna remember my last meal, either." He smiled sheepishly. "Takes a grand lot to keep me going."

She smiled back, holding out the sandwich plate. "Eat." She loved the way his expression turned eager, eyes sparkling with the grin.

Finally at ease, he sighed deeply and sat back on the couch with his long legs stretched before him. While she poured more coffee, he said, "Satisfy m'curiosity and tell me how a young lass turns racing jockey."

She shrugged. "My father was a jock. He

taught me, and on the track you get addicted early."

"Yer father? My God, it's so dangerous." Clearly, Connor was shocked. "And now you've made it a lifelong occupation, what does he think?"

Alix looked away casually. "He died when I was still a bug."

In the process of taking a sip of coffee, Connor knocked his teeth against the china rim. He steadied the cup before asking, "I beg yer pardon?"

"Oh." Alix smiled, realizing he wasn't up on racetrack jargon. "A bug is an apprentice jockey."

He nodded thoughtfully.

"And you, Connor." She broke a quiet that had gone on too long. "How did you end up in California?"

His head jerked up, and she was caught by the look in his dark eyes. Something flashed, then it was replaced by blankness.

"I . . . got started in medicine late," he began slowly. "Then I was offered a residency in the States. But I soon tired of New York and wanted to be somewhere smaller, quieter."

She loved the way his accent came and went like flashes of color. She wondered if he knew how clearly he displayed his emotions by its presence, or absence.

"You . . . live on my street?" She had to struggle to make conversation. All she really wanted to do was look at him. But there was no future in that.

"I rent a house from a friend. It's just a way down, actually. Gray weathered shingles, red mailbox . . ."

"I know the one. Nice place."

She couldn't help it. She looked into his eyes and wanted to know. "Do you have kids, Connor?" She tried to ask casually, but she thought it still sounded predatory.

"No," he answered, but he seemed more interested in his coffee. "Not married. Are you?"

"Oh, no."

"Why not?" He was surprised. "Ah, I forget, ye're s'young. American women stay single much longer now." He knew it was daft, but he wanted this girl. There was something deep in her eyes, an honest sweetness and something else. The way she looked at him . . . pulled him to her.

"Mmm," Alix answered noncommittally, then changed the subject. "You like being a doctor, don't you, Connor? You seem to . . . care a great deal." She saw one side of his beautiful, sculpted mouth slide upward at that.

"Well,'tis . . . part of my business." He shifted, and his muscles moved under the fine white shirt.

"Oh." She blushed, looking down into her coffee. "Stupid question."

He reached out and lifted her chin. His hand was warm as he growled, "Not a bit. I see a fine lot of doctors who've become mere technicians." His hand dropped away. "What will you do while you're out of commission?"

She wrinkled her nose in distaste. "That's the worst. I have to spend most of my time working out, so I'll be ready to go right back when the cast is off. And—I hate to run, but I'll be doing it."

"Dinna overdo the first week." He was the doctor again, and she fashioned a mock salute in answer.

"Well." He rubbed at the back of his neck again. "I'd better be goin' along afore I fall asleep on yer sofa."

She couldn't help it, she'd never been able to resist anything in pain. "Look, Con. You could take two aspirin, but I think I could do something about that neck. Acupressure, you know?"

He looked surprised, off guard. He studied

her for a minute, then said, "Think you can do it with one hand?"

She smiled. "Piece o' cake."

A strange moment passed then, a moment that changed the air around them in a way she couldn't pinpoint. She jumped when he sighed.

"It's been plaguin' me for the last six or seven hours."

"Just sit back so I can reach you." She walked around to the back of the couch and perched sideways for the best angle. Looking down, she could see his gentle brow, the chiseled plane of his fine nose, and the full curve of his lips. She put her hand on the side of his neck.

Warm. His skin felt alive and so warm. His shoulders were impossibly wide, and the thick muscles there flexed as he sat back and settled himself.

"I think you'd better get this off." She reached around him for the knot of his tie. He tensed at the touch of her shaky hand. Their fingers brushed as he helped.

Finally, the tie was loose enough to pull over his head, then Connor unbuttoned his collar. She moved again and felt his hair, spun silk, sliding against her fingers. That heated skin was smooth, and he smelled of man and fresh sea air.

Alix took a deep breath. She felt strange, almost as if she were outside herself, with the craziest urge to put her lips to the nape of that sleek, corded neck.

Making a face at herself, she thought that women must flock to a man like this. It was embarrassing that she wanted to be one of them.

"Here." Her voice had a husky sound to it she tried to control. "I think this is it."

He groaned in acknowledgment, and she swallowed at the sound.

"I'll just knead it lightly until I can find the worst. Ah, there. Now, there might be a pinch when I press the pressure point, but then it'll feel much better. Okay, here goes." She felt him tense against her fingers. "Try to relax, Connor. Take a deep breath. Out . . . Then another." His thick, shining curls caught the light. "There, feel that? It's going."

He could feel it, all right. Her hand was doing wild things to his heart rate. It had been a long time since he'd felt the softness of a woman's touch. And the pain was going away at last. He sighed and closed his eyes. "Aye. Lovely."

Alix had to laugh. He was putty in her hands—for a moment.

"There you go," she said, and reluctantly took

her hand away. He stretched slowly, like a great, dark animal, while Alix stared.

"Thanks." He reached up to test her work, and his fingers brushed against hers, startling them both. "Ah, that's grand."

She walked back around to her chair and grabbed for her coffee. "It's a talent, that," he said, looking her over warmly.

She grinned back. "Works on horses." Then she heard the phone ring. " 'Scuse me."

It was Sammy, her agent.

"Sure, I'm fine. No big deal, Sammy," she said in answer to his concerns. "Yeah, it's just . . . What did you say? . . . How?"

Connor watched the sprite turn to tough pro in an instant and raised a brow. Whatever her Sammy was saying, she didn't like it.

"How much damage to Pride? Okay . . ." She seemed to slump. "How could it happen, Sammy, and why? I weighed in with my chamois, but I don't know if we used mine or the barn's in the end. Did you talk to the valet?" She shook her head, frowning. "No, no, I'm fine. I'll be riding again in two weeks. But will you get somebody to go pick up my car at the hospital? Keys are behind the visor. I got a ride home."

Connor listened unashamedly as she said her

good-byes. There was affection in her voice, but any more than that was hard to tell.

"Trouble, lass?" he asked.

She was staring blankly at a wall, deep in thought. At his question she walked slowly to the windows and looked out. "No," she answered. "Just something that happened at the track, something strange."

"Strange," he repeated, encouraging more.

When she turned toward him, her eyes were fierce and a little sad. "Someone put a piece of barbed wire in my saddle chamois. That must have been the cause of Pride's tantrum."

Connor frowned. "That could have been a very serious accident, couldn't it?"

She wrapped her arms around herself and nodded. "Things happen occasionally, vandalism or bad jokes . . . but this . . ."

"And the horse?" he asked, watching her closely.

"Just some scratches, Sammy says. A day or two and those'll heal. But they've alerted track security, and the trainer is checking his grooms."

"Are you all right?" Connor stood and walked over to her. "Not shaky at the news? I can stay if you want."

Alix shook her head, surprised at the offer.

Did she look like she was about to fall apart? "Thanks, but no. Just one of those things, I guess. They'll be on the lookout now."

"Well," he said, "I thank you for the healing, the food, and the company."

She watched him put his jacket, tie, and coat over his arm and head for the door. She followed, telling herself it was best that he leave. She'd probably run out of small talk anyway.

At the door, Connor looked down at her. It was selfish, but he couldn't just walk away from her. She aroused his senses in a way he hadn't felt for years. "I . . . Can I see you again? For supper?"

Alix blinked, swallowed. "Yes."

"Good." He smiled and his face lit. "How is Sunday night, then?"

"All right." A coquette she wasn't.

He leaned down and brushed his lips across hers before she even had time to panic at the thought. It was electric, that touch. Intrigued, he tested it again. Once, twice, and then his lips settled warmly upon hers. A shudder went through her, and her knees buckled right out from under her.

Connor caught her around the waist and she dragged herself back, eyes still closed. Both of them were breathing fast and the tension was thick in the air.

Finally, Alix shook her head and lifted shocked eyes to his. "Connor," she started, then had no idea where to go from there.

"Aye, lass?" His voice trickled through her, weakening her knees once more. His hands barely touched her arms, but they froze her in place. Her mouth moved twice before sound came.

"Nothing." She looked down at his shiny shoes.

"Sunday, then," he said before he brushed a wisp of hair from her face and let himself out.

Shameless, Alix kept the door open a crack and watched until his long legs were all the way up the steps and the gate closed behind him.

TWO

Inside the vast, dark-paneled office overlooking the Charles River, Bentley Barstow threw the report he'd been studying across the room, narrowly missing a Greek bowl that predated Christ by a thousand years. Turning to the window, his hands fisted upon his hips, he decided that the only way to get a job done was to do it himself.

Bentley was lean and blond in a charcoal Versace suit. Women were attracted to his boyish looks and rich man's toys. The family business had brought him important friends. But there was something behind his green eyes that was repellent, a slyness he usually kept masked.

When his mother died earlier that year, Bentley had thought he would finally have it all. No more allowance, no more trust fund. But when he found the papers detailing the family holdings, he had learned that the family fortune belonged, in fact, to his sweet little cousin—who now called herself Alix—on her twenty-fifth birthday. All of the thirty-five million dollars he had waited for so very patiently. After giving his life to the family business of banking and real estate, he was to receive only the Boston house and the paltry seven million his mother had left him.

He had gone into a rage that day that hadn't been soothed until he'd broken his mistress's collarbone and blackened one of her eyes. Of course, Natalya had made certain that his bit of temper had cost him. But, he thought, lip curling, it had been worth it to feel the satisfaction that came from allowing his temper free rein.

Pushing a button on his phone he said, "Marie, have them ready the jet this afternoon. I'm taking a vacation for two weeks. Cancel all my appointments. Oh, and have Tiffany's overnight something to Natalya. Five-thousand-dollar range, usual card."

The clinic's emergency room was crazy the next day. Muñiz gave orders like a general and took guff from nobody.

Connor glanced up at the worried face of the

fifteen-year-old football player he was tending.

"Just a splint for support, lad, and you'll be right in a few weeks." He was grateful the boy had only sprained his arm. The jockeys were his easiest patients; they were used to pain and their injuries were mostly minor. The tough cases were the old people without the money to take care of problems until they were critical. Then there were the children, hurt and frightened, whom Muñiz always made sure saw him.

When he finished with the football player, Muñiz took him aside. "Timmy here slipped onto the track to watch the jockeys' morning workout. But he got too close to one of the horses with temperament and got a solid kick for his trouble. He didn't want his mother to know he had gone to the track, so he didn't tell anyone he was hurt for more than two hours."

Connor looked at the boy and nodded. The boy was sitting in a wheelchair next to his worried young mother, both of them trying to hold back tears. Connor hunkered down beside the wheelchair, so they were eye to eye.

"Hallo, Timmy, I'm Dr. Connor. Are you the lad who did battle with the wild stallion?"

"He kicked me." The boy's lower lip trembled. "I only wanted to pet him."

"Och, laddie." Connor's scowl melted to a tender look and he ruffled the boy's hair. "The beast was a wee bit nervous. He wouldna have hurt ye apurpose."

"He was so beautiful . . . shiny and . . . great big eyes . . ."

"Well, suppose we see ye have another chance." He leaned close and whispered, "I know a lady jockey who might be convinced to let ye an' me pat one of those great shiny horses." Timmy's face lit up and Connor went on. "Now, come with me and we'll investigate the damage."

Children had always been special to him, although he had avoided them for years. Sorcha had been responsible for that.

"It's my leg got hurt," Timmy said importantly.

"Well, I know that." Connor looked down disdainfully as he took his place behind the wheelchair. "I'm the doctor, you know," he said as he began to push the chair. And somehow, for no reason at all, Timmy giggled and Connor grinned.

Alix got her cast the next day, but there was no sign of Connor at the clinic.

She spent Saturday afternoon with her friend Dani and a few kids from up the block. They played a wide-dash version of Frisbee football.

Later, she and Dani grabbed a sandwich at Solley's. More than just a friend, Dani was her favorite ponygirl at the track. Riding with a lead line attached to Alix's horse during the post parade, she could be trusted to keep them at a reasonable pace so Alix's horse didn't run the race before the bell.

They discussed the barbed wire incident and tossed back ideas as to who might have had the opportunity. The "why" baffled both of them.

Alix came home happy, before she remembered that tomorrow night she had a date.

Of course, maybe it wasn't a date at all. Maybe it was really just an invitation to be some sort of androgynous dinner companion for a man who was lonely and far from his home. But whatever it was—and whatever he wanted—she wasn't backing away from that brawny, dark-haired Scot.

For the first time since she was fifteen years old, she had no fear of a man's touch. Of course, she was suffering another kind of panic. She had no idea what to wear.

*   *   *

She decided on a dress. She had them, after all. So what if it was a pale, feminine peach color? That didn't mean she was trying for Miss North Carolina, did it?

It was silk, body-hugging silk, that flowed and fell against her slight curves as she moved. It made much of what she hardly had.

She knew she might be taking a chance, but she had decided she'd lived in shadows long enough. She had decided this risk was worth the gamble.

Connor had never seen her in a skirt. She wasn't a tall woman, only five feet four, but that still made her tower over most of the jocks. She had long legs, though, and they were well displayed with this dress.

She took a final look in the bathroom mirror and stared hard. Her eyes looked wide and more blue than green. Her face was flushed with excitement, and her hair fell in a dark blond mass over her shoulders and down her back. She tried to school her features into some expression that didn't look so apprehensive, but it was difficult.

By the time he arrived, she was nearly sick to her stomach. She'd been pacing the living room for fourteen minutes when she heard the bell.

Breathe. Breathe!

She'd left the outside gate propped open and, looking through the peephole, she saw a right shoulder covered in a tweed jacket. She angled over for the reassurance of the tie he always wore. Up, and there was the hard nose and the sight of one chocolate eye, downcast. The lashes were as thick and beguiling as a four year old's.

She allowed herself one sigh, then stood up straight. Her hand fumbled with the lock, then there he was, the whole great height of him, at her door.

"Ah," he said, staring, "but ye're a lovely thing, lass."

Alix grinned in disbelief. He'd pulled wildly for that one. Still, she thought, turning her face to hide the softening in her eyes, it was nice to have a man call her lovely.

When she glanced back, it was her turn to stare. What she hadn't seen through the peephole was his hand, and the violets held in it.

Connor watched her mouth go round and soft, and thought how glad he was for the violets. He wanted badly to tease her, at least enough so that she would look at him. The moment was precious and fine, though, and he let her collect herself before he gave them to her.

She made a funny little noise in her throat before she squeaked out her thanks, then she turned on her heel to find a vase for the flowers.

He followed her into the living room and stared at her long, beautiful, delicate legs as she walked on to the kitchen. He smiled at the craziness of it. Her ankles actually made his heart change rhythm, and pictures filled his mind of kissing the back of those tender knees. He wanted to see what it would do to those blue-green eyes when he touched her.

Enough, he commanded himself, closing his eyes. He lifted his jaw and made his way to the windows.

For years his emotions had all been poured into his work. Sorcha had destroyed any vulnerability he might have had. He thought she had demolished his ability to feel as well. Why now? He turned back to look toward the kitchen. What was it about this sweet, fey young thing that made him feel again?

He hadn't had much to do with women since Sorcha. Hadn't been with one in a while, a long while. Since his wife, there hadn't been many, and they had been women who looked at him as if he were something they had just found at a sales promotion.

Truth be told, that was fine with him. He hadn't wanted more than to sate his body and take comfort from theirs, to share a bit of human warmth. A man needed that.

But Alix . . . He saw that he could hurt her. He wanted her anyway, wanted something that she had, something she gave without thinking. Maybe it was the honesty, that lack of pretense, or maybe it was just that startled look she got, like it was the first time anyone had ever really looked at her.

God, she was sweet, her eyes so full of feeling. He wanted to run his hands over her and find every delicate curve, bury himself in her softness. He felt clumsy next to her smallness.

He felt the worst kind of idiot poet.

Alix came into the room and set the small glass vase filled with his violets upon the coffee table. When she straightened, he was looking at her so darkly, her smile became uncertain.

He announced quickly, "I made reservations at a place recommended by a friend. Will you chance it?" The dark look faded from his eyes as he smiled.

"Sure."

A moment passed, then he said, "Ye've bonnie hair."

This time she believed him and smiled shyly.

He took her to a place that looked like an old European hunting lodge. They ate French food and drank wine, and Alix learned as much as Connor would talk about.

He was from the Isle of Skye. He'd grown up one of three children. He'd been a wild adolescent, always "in the rough," played football—"Rugby, to you Americans"—to get through college, then worked an oil rig. There, he saw accidents and found himself powerless to help. A few years later he decided to study medicine in the States, "to the everlasting dismay of family and all who knew me."

After that, his life was school, more school, cadavers and diagnoses, and finally, a residency in New York. When the chance came to open this clinic with four other doctors, he grabbed it.

"You didn't like New York," she said, knowing from the way he had spoken about it that he hadn't.

He made a jerky movement with his head. "Too much gray, too little green." Then he looked at her. "I like it here," he said as if that might redeem him.

"I've never been to New York, but there are a lot of New Yorkers who come to California. I think they must like it better too." Suddenly, she asked, "You've never been married?"

His eyes pinned her, all softness gone. "Aye, I was."

"What happened?" she whispered, thinking it must have been terrible to make him look like that.

"I was a fool," he answered shortly, his eyes as flat as pennies, "married to a liar."

"Oh." Her voice was very small. "She hurt you." She reached for his hand on the tabletop and covered it with hers. "I'm sorry."

Connor smiled and turned his hand to hold hers. He asked her what it was like growing up around the racetrack. She told him about her father, Boots, who had taught her everything, and Sammy, her agent. Sammy was as tough as they came with forty years in the business, but he had a soft spot for horses and girls named Alix who he thought needed looking after.

"Did they find out anything more about the vandal?" he asked, happy to learn Sammy's identity.

"Nope." She shook her head, and he watched the candlelight play over her skin, aching to test its softness. "I've been winning a lot of races lately. I guess somebody had a reason to make sure Pride didn't run that day. It'll be forgotten next week."

After dinner, he took her home, and Alix asked him in for coffee. He looked immense, sprawled out on her couch. The sight made her happy somehow.

Feeling self-conscious, she put on quiet music, turned down the lights, and they looked at the stars through the glass doors. Alix's head fell back against the couch and she sighed in contentment. Her home had never felt so warm and comfortable.

Connor put his elbow on the back of the couch, bracing his head in his hand as he looked at her. He thought her hair looked moonspun as it lay across the fringed pillows.

"I thought I could wait, but I canna." His voice deepened as he stared down into her fairy face. "Nae longer." His hand slid, so slowly, through strands of hair at the nape of her neck. "I mean," he continued in a gravel voice, "I'm dyin' away to kiss ye, lass."

Alix closed her eyes at the luxury of his words,

at the way they made her feel. She didn't care if he said things like this to every woman he met. He was saying them to her.

His hand massaged her nape and she shivered. Her chin lifted, lips parting. This time his lips met her mouth fully, in a kiss both warm and soft. Connor smiled at the sweetness of her taste, and his tongue came out to flick her upper lip.

She gave a reckless sound of longing, and he deepened the kiss, delving between her lips with his warm tongue.

Alix could feel her heart thundering against his chest, but miraculously, there was no ice, no fear. He pulled her closer to his hard body, and her hands pressed into his shoulders, fingers curling, the cast an encumbrance.

His hands smoothed up and down her back, slowly sliding heat against fabric, feeling every rib and fine muscle. She felt enveloped in that heat. The longing in it swept through her.

Never had she felt so much a woman.

His fingers were entangled in her hair, cupping the sides of her jaw through it, rubbing its silk over her cheeks in a way that made her gasp as he moved her the way he wanted. She began to tremble.

It went on and on, the kiss completely stunning, until she couldn't breathe at all, couldn't see, couldn't think. Then he pulled away, nibbling with his lips over her cheekbones, and moved slowly down the slender column of her throat as she gasped for air and held on to his head.

His hand rose to her breast and cupped it tenderly, just where it ached, brushing tantalizingly over the hardened nipple until her knees knocked restlessly against his.

She gave a little shudder of arousal . . . and he stopped. His hand was motionless upon her breast, his knee lay between hers, his mouth stilled at her collarbone.

Her eyes flew open and she couldn't breathe.

"N'more," he whispered harshly.

"No more . . ."

Bewildered, heart still pounding, Alix felt him draw away from her, until they no longer touched anywhere. She wanted to cry out at the loss, to beg him to kiss her again. But there had been a strangeness in his voice she didn't understand. And now it was on his face as she looked at him.

Why? Why had he stopped?

She waited, but he didn't speak, just closed his eyes tight and got his breath back. Finally, when she couldn't stand not knowing anymore, she turned her head away and asked, "I . . . umm, did I . . . do something . . . ?" She couldn't finish, the words wouldn't come.

His eyes opened, and he rested the curl of his fist under her chin to turn her to him. His skin was flushed and his lips seemed more full. He melted her with his chocolate stare.

"Ye're a silly clunch, ye are." His voice was hoarse and tender now, and he sighed. "I . . . promised myself that I'd no more than kiss ye, lass. That I'd give ye proper time. But ye . . . I . . ." He shook his head and explained no more. Even so, his words made everything right again.

He looked at her, and one corner of his mouth lifted. "Walk me to your door?"

She rose with him and led the way, watching her feet. He opened the door. Deciding she was being a coward, she turned, at last, to face him. She asked no more questions, though, because she was still afraid of the answers.

"Good night." The back of his fingers brushed her cheek. She opened her mouth to say good night, and he said, "I'll no' forget."

No. No questions, she ordered herself. Have a little dignity, just let him go.

But when he turned away she called to him. "Connor?" His eyes met hers, and she walked the three steps he'd taken. She hesitated before reaching up to smooth the hair she'd mussed over his forehead. Then she smiled her good-bye. He smiled back.

Alix thought about him every day after that. Wondering what she might have done, should have done, differently. Once she even thought she saw him at the track. She was there to talk to security and ask the stablehands a few questions. She looked at the Double D barn and saw a big man round the corner with his head bent. She froze, but then the man turned and she saw it wasn't Connor at all.

Just wishful thinking, she scolded herself. How would he have gotten backside? Besides, the man hadn't even worn a suit, much less a tie.

She was a slave to her answering machine, checking it too often.

By Wednesday afternoon, she was angry at herself. It had been a long time since she had regretted her boyish ways and boyish body. It was what she was, after all.

And she had tried, one humiliating time, to play the girlie girl.

Walking to the glass doors of her living room, she pushed them open and let the cool breeze flow over her and into the house. Then she stepped to the railing of her redwood deck. Standing with her head back, hair flying in the soft wind, she let memory flow over her in the same cool rush, this time without all of the pain, without the humiliation.

She hadn't been strictly truthful when she told Connor her father was a jockey. She did think of Boots as her father. But he was her chosen father, not her natural one. He was the one who had first noticed the puny, hungry-looking kid mucking out stalls for food and board at Hollywood Park. He had gotten her a job as an exercise girl at the Santa Anita Racetrack and given her a room in his own house. Later, when she trusted him enough to tell him her story, he called an ex-cop buddy who showed her how to be safe. He told her exactly how to get the copy of a birth certificate of a dead girl born a year before her and present it to the DMV for a new identity. It might have been illegal, but without the reassurance that no one could come after her, Alix would surely have moved on, probably to the streets of Hollywood.

Her real father had died in a plane crash

along with her mother when she was seven, leaving her widowed aunt as her guardian.

She had never understood why Maud and she were always at odds. Maybe it was because her aunt had a rule for all occasions and Alix had never had a rule in her life before. They battled every issue, and Maud's punishments only made Alix more stubborn.

Because Maud was Beacon Hill silk and pearls, Alix was the grimiest, most foulmouthed tomboy ever to disgrace a dinner table. Unlike Bentley, Maud's perfect son, Alix was sent to bed without dinner so often, she probably would have starved to death by the age of ten if Roberts-the-butler and Daphne-the-cook hadn't had such a good system of sneaking her food.

Bentley was three years older than she, and she learned to hate and despise him in the space of a few days' time. Oh yes, he was a perfect gentleman in every way, except when there was no audience. Then he would bully anything smaller than himself, namely, Catherine Eugenie Barstow, now Alixandra Benton.

From the day she arrived, alone and forlorn, Bentley made no effort to disguise his hostility. At first, it was only little things, like frogs and garden snakes in her room. But Alix had played in her mother's garden since she could walk. When she showed no reaction, he took his mother's favorite dress and slashed it to ribbons before hiding it in Alix's dresser.

Maud used a belt on her and made her stand in the corner for three hours as punishment.

Later that summer, she found Bentley shooting squirrels with his BB gun. A physical battle would have been ridiculous; he was older and a great deal bigger. But when Bentley wouldn't stop, she finally went to Maud. Her aunt smiled dismissingly and said it was only a boyish prank. The next day he used that gun to blind Alix's terrier in one eye.

Bentley found her cradling the little dog in the backyard. Walking up to her, he put a cold finger to the tear that had slipped down one cheek and bent to her ear. "You got more stories to tell, little cat?" he whispered. "Okay. But you think about Spinner. Such a little dog."

She looked into cold green eyes that promised all things terrible. Alix never said another word against him to anyone.

Fortunately, when she was twelve, she was sent away to school. She rarely saw Bentley again until the night she turned fifteen. The night she ran away.

But that was long ago.

Anyway, she had a goal, didn't she? A million dollars to fund her own stable. That should be the only thing on her mind.

She went back inside and called Dani to come over and work out. She had a use for this quiet fury inside her.

They pushed themselves to the limit for three hours, until Alix was limp spaghetti without a thought in her head. Finally, tiny, dark-haired Dani grabbed a towel and staggered to the stereo to punch off the music.

"Murder!" she exclaimed. "It was hamstring abuse, Your Honor! Her muscles swelled until they burst!" Dani wheeled around, gesturing dramatically. "What, you're afraid I'll tell the other jocks your bra size? What other reason you got for trying to kill me!"

Alix caught the towel Dani tossed her way, laughing. "I'm thinking."

"Well, give it up,'cause I'm going home to soak my achin' body. Not that I don't appreciate how miserable I'll be tomorrow." She smirked and slipped her bulky cotton sweater over her head. "If I come back, it's because I found that old Girl Scout knife I lost last year in my glove compartment an' I'm comin' after you."

"No!" Alix held her stomach, laughing soundlessly. "I'm too sore to laugh, but, oh, I like the picture of you stalking me with a Girl Scout knife between your teeth! I'll drag myself to the door if that'll get you out of here and me into a hot shower."

"You know," Dani was suddenly serious. "You could just tell me what's bugging you."

Alix smiled and cocked her head as she answered, "I think it'll go away faster if I don't."

"Okay." Dani shrugged lightly. "Use me, abuse me, and throw me out."

Alix stuck out her tongue and Dani returned the favor. Then they mock-staggered to the door together, and after she'd closed it behind Dani, Alix leaned against the cool wood.

Her body was drenched and her head light. Her muscles quivered with every move. She called herself ten times a fool for overdoing it as she groaned and pushed away from the door, heading for the fridge and the Gatorade.

Drinking straight from the bottle, she heard echoes of Aunt Maud and felt sinful and decadent. She was wiping her face with the towel around her neck as the doorbell rang.

She couldn't think who it could be. Sammy was out of town. She stumbled to the door and released the gate, then grinned. It could only be Dani, coming to show her she'd found the Girl Scout knife.

She swung open the door, wiping her face again with one end of the towel, and found a hundred pounds more than she'd expected. Giving a startled squawk, she lifted her gaze past the eye-level chest and quiet tie to the happy look on Connor's face.

She, on the other hand, wore a sweat-soaked, skintight two-piece aqua spandex thing that covered two inches more than a bikini . . . and a look of horror.

THREE

"I'm glad I didna take the time to call." Connor stepped past her and looked her over again. He had a brown grocery bag in one arm, and it was stuffed full of something.

"You . . . are?" she asked stiffly.

"I canna abide the telephone," he growled in typical fashion. "I'm chained to it in my work." Then, just when she was certain she could stir up enough anger to kick him out, he gave half a grin and said, "N'fear, lassie. I well know I'm in trouble here."

She turned away. She could hardly laugh and command him to leave at the same time.

"Then what are you doing here?" She looked up, way up. Why did he have to be such a beautiful man?

"I couldna help m'self." He looked serious, so

lovely and serious. "I've been at the clinic, double shift the last few days. We're short staffed from the flu."

He gave her a look that sent a small maelstrom through her, then he leaned near. "An' every time I slip home to sleep, I pass yer house. An' I know if I knock at yer door, I wouldna get back to the clinic in six hours . . . or twelve."

Good line! she thought angrily. Of course, it had only been three days. But any American man would know to cement a first date with a phone call. She considered him. Well, he wasn't an American, was he? Alix bit her lip in indecision.

"Connor," she said, keeping her voice a monotone. "I like to know the rules of play up front. I'm not much for after-the-fact explanation."

He raised a gentle hand to her cheek, sliding his thumb over her jaw. "But 'tis no game I'm playin', lass."

She was mush.

He paused and stared into her eyes. "You have every right to be angry with me. An' I do wish to make amends."

"Amends," she repeated. Studying him, she cocked one brow. "How do you plan to do that?"

That pleased him, there was no doubt. "I

c'n make ye dinner, if ye let me. I have a few specialties."

His arrogance was so entertaining, she wanted to laugh again. Instead, she asked straight-faced, "Pigs' intestines, cows' brains, and other Scottish treats?"

"Possibly," he said sternly. "But I would prefer," he added with a wicked look, "you tasted the fare afore you criticized."

"Neatly done, Doctor. You've invited yourself in . . . and to dinner." She tugged on both ends of the towel around her neck as she walked to the bedroom. At the door, she tossed over her shoulder, "You must think you're awfully good."

The door closed behind her, and Connor fortified himself with a deep breath and a satisfied smile. The chase was on.

Closing his eyes, he could still see her. Her body was neat, compact, that of an athlete. But her breasts were rounded and beautiful, her waist so small. Her hips, thighs, and the sweet, plump curve of her bottom were well defined. The sight had made him want her badly . . . instantly.

Yes, he wanted her, and he thanked heaven for the feeling. It had been too long since he had felt anything so strong, so real.

*   *   *

Alix showered and pulled a long red sweater on over her jeans. Really, it was silly to be this nervous over a simple dinner, and in her own home! But for some crazy reason, she had this incredible reaction to the mere sight of him.

Connor was a companionable man in the kitchen, although she had to note, he did take up space.

First, he insisted on examining her hand. When he had assured himself that he was satisfied with the job they had done on her fiberglass cast, he rubbed her fingertips with the pad of his thumb. It wasn't smooth, the way you'd expect a doctor's hand to be. There were calluses, thick and years old; the hands of a working man.

He turned abruptly to rummage in her cabinets, leaving her standing like a statue.

Coming back to the real world and physical motion, Alix made her way to the refrigerator and pulled out salad fixings. As she chopped she pretended not to watch him.

He requested opera "for proper ambience," then made her laugh as he conducted. Who would have thought her scowling doctor would open up like this?

He had brought spaghetti, for her "weight problem," he announced.

"I don't have a weight problem," she said, looking at the mountain of pasta he dumped into her biggest pot, "but I will if I eat that."

"Hmm," he said thoughtfully as he turned. He grasped her waist and lifted her high, as if she weighed no more than a mouse. Startled, she grabbed his broad shoulders, clumsy with the cast. "Mmmhmm." He grinned and pulled her closer, rearranging his arms until she lay against his wide chest, feet dangling. One hand braced her bottom, and she gasped in shocked delight.

"Well . . ." He gave her a squeeze there— that was definitely a squeeze. "The proportion is right, but the scale tells me ye need . . . a pound of spaghetti covered with rich red sauce." His voice slowed, caressing each word. "With plum tomatoes and red peppers, garlic and sweet . . . basil." He let her slide slowly down his muscular body to the floor while she remained speechless.

"Have ye ground pepper?" he asked casually.

Connor tried not to laugh as, still staring at him, she backed away and reached behind her for the pepper mill. She knocked it sideways, then steadied it. Their fingers brushed as she handed it to him. Alix turned away, swallowing hard. She could still feel the shape of him as she returned to chopping vegetables. She had felt the warm, rounded muscles of his chest, the cords and sinews of his great thighs. He was the strongest man she'd ever seen. He had also been aroused. She shot him a sidelong glance. Very aroused.

The pasta was wonderful, but she couldn't eat much. Too nervous. He ate three platefuls and looked disparagingly at hers. Tearing off another piece of bread, he said, "You dinna like it."

"Oh no," she protested, twirling another bite hastily. "It's wonderful. Really. Great." She tried to sound ecstatic, or at least look it as she chewed.

Connor grinned and stared at the drop of sauce at the corner of her mouth. Her tongue flicked out to catch it. There was still a dot left behind, and he reached out to dab at it with his finger.

She looked embarrassed, until he put his tongue to his finger and licked it off. Her pupils widened and her breasts rose and fell quickly. His smile turned wicked.

Dinner was over.

He wiped his mouth and laid his napkin on the table as he rose. He reached out a hand, palm up, for hers. Puccini played heartbreakingly in the background. Alix could barely breathe. Her hand rose . . . and her fingers touched his.

She should tell him, she thought. What if she couldn't do it?

But he was looking at her with such warm caring, and hunger behind that, she was left without words.

He pulled her up to stand before him and cradled her face in his hands. Bending, he pressed solemn lips to her eyes, her brows, her cheeks. Soon, she was searching upward for his mouth, her hands flat against his crisp shirt.

Her fingers had become so sensitized, she could feel everything—the heat of his body, the fine texture of his shirt, the hint of chest muscles beneath. Finally, his mouth found hers and she sighed. He smiled, right there where she could feel it. He lifted her high in his arms and she gasped. He was wasting no more time! He carried her into her almost-neat bedroom and let her slide down his body once more.

Alix shivered, and his kisses deepened, his hands roved. He bit her lips, lightly, teasingly, and groaned as his tongue found hers. She felt dizzy at the touch of that tongue and let hers play against it in wonder at the sensations produced. His hands roamed her back from shoulders to hips and down, and she suddenly panicked. Should she tell him? How could she tell him? Just start talking, she thought.

"A doctor," she murmured between kisses. "So . . . this is probably all very clinical to you . . ."

The left corner of his mouth twitched. "Not that you would notice." He was trying not to pant.

"You probably see hundreds of bodies every day." She gasped as his mouth found her ear. "Voluptuous . . . ah . . ." She was surprised by something; it was his tongue. "Tall." She turned her head, giving him better access. "Soft." She smiled. Yes, that place on her neck made her smile. "Bodies. Um . . . hundreds."

"Ah, lassie," he breathed against her skin, "touching you makes me . . . quite wild." He grazed the skin behind her ear with his tongue. "You smell so feminine and sweet. Ye're soft . . ."

She made a quiet sound of derision, but it stopped when she felt the warmth of his hand upon her small breast. Her body responded instantly.

"And so verra delicate." His brogue thickened as his hand traced down around her waist and over her bottom.

He growled, very low, as he squeezed her there. "Here." His hand traveled farther over her taut, jean-encased thighs and inward. "And here," he sighed.

His mouth met hers at the moment she might have protested the intimacy, and her cry was caught. Her senses reeled and she reached for his neck.

Then a strange sound came from nowhere, making her fingers jerk back and her cast knock his jaw.

His beeper, she finally realized. There was a frozen moment, then Alix shot out of his arms while Connor ground his teeth and threw back his head, eyes closed in frustration.

"The phone's . . . over there." She pointed to a bedside table before she ran for the bathroom. Once inside, she stared in the mirror, hardly recognizing herself.

Opera and ties and umbrellas! she thought, both horrified and mesmerized.

She looked again at the mirror. Her face was flushed, her lips full, and she felt a swollen aching between her thighs. He wanted her, and she was very much afraid he knew just how much she wanted him. It had been in his eyes.

When she came out, he was putting on his coat.

"I have to go," he said quietly. His eyes searched her face as she nodded.

"Dinner was terrific." She tried to say more, but faltered.

"I dinna ken how long it may take," he continued.

"Of course."

He looked at her then, until she was forced to look back.

"It's all going a might fast, isn't it," he said in a low voice, "this thing between us?"

The silence strung out. "Yes," she finally answered.

"It's been a long time for me," he said, his eyes burning her. "And the way I feel, I'm not certain I can slow it down."

Alix gulped and murmured, "Mmm." Great vocabulary, she chastised herself.

He took it for agreement and smiled, pleased. "I will no' kiss ye now. Because if I do, I wilna go."

That made her ridiculously disappointed, ridiculously happy.

"Come back if you can," she whispered.

He opened his arms for her and she ran to him. His warmth enfolded her, and Alix was overwhelmed with the security of it, the peace. She felt cherished in a way she'd never felt before. Her fingers pressed against his chest, and she turned a kiss to the place she could feel his heart thumping.

"Och, Alix." He groaned before he bent to take her mouth, despite his best intentions. "Dreadful hard to leave . . ." He groaned again as his tongue swept past her lips, searching every secret, every taste.

Alix whimpered and grasped a handful of his shirt in response. But then his mouth was gone and he was crushing her to him, only to let her go.

By the time she opened her eyes, she was alone.

Connor rushed through the automatic doors of the ER.

It was a war zone—cacophony, rolling gurneys, shouted orders, cries of pain. There were broken limbs, multiple burns, concussions, contusions, and rivers of blood.

Muñiz lost no time updating him. All available bodies had been called in, every moment was vital.

A school bus on the way to a basketball game had collided with a semi and burst into flames. Twenty junior high school students were injured, two were dead. The clinic was closer than the hospital.

He tossed his jacket in a corner as Muñiz briefed him on his first patient. It was a red-headed boy, only eleven or twelve. His aorta was punctured and he was in full arrest.

Connor got to work. "All right, let's get some more lines into him. I want to open him up."

An hour passed, two, then the ER was clear. Many of the staff hovered, waiting for word from surgery. Sitting in the lounge in bloody greens or street clothes, they sipped thin coffee from wilting paper cups. Nothing like this had ever come through the clinic before, and the air snapped with emotion.

Finally, case after case, the news trickled in to them. After four hours, eighteen of those admitted were still alive, three in intensive care.

With the last bit of information, weary smiles and awkward hugs went around. Then they pushed through the swinging doors to the hallway, past the press, to share their feelings with the families who had received the same news.

Connor stayed, fingers pinching the bridge of his nose, his mind crowded with images of the last few hours. He and Muñiz had worked together on the two kids who had died, the first redheaded boy and a girl with a head injury. The eyes of the parents of those children haunted him.

He had lost patients before, and each loss hurt. Sometimes they took days to get over. But for some reason, everything seemed different this night. For Connor, it was a revelation and a warning. Life was sweet and it was bitter.

Life was short.

He looked up when Muñiz touched his arm.

"Home," she said quietly, understanding the injured look in his dark eyes.

Alix sat straight up in bed. There it was again, a creaking sound, like footsteps. Throwing back the sheet, she walked through her dark bedroom, heart pounding.

In the living room, she pushed a corner of the drapes aside. Connor stood on her deck, his two hands spread wide on the glass doors, head down, rain pouring over him. She gave a soft cry of alarm and wrenched the lock open, then the door.

She had no chance to pull him inside. He dragged her out into the rain and into his arms. He was shaking as he held her tightly. "Alix," he whispered hoarsely.

Water coursed over them both, flattening his sable curls to his head, making thick, wet spikes of his long lashes. In an instant, her hair was in long ropes and her nightshirt clung to every curve.

"Connor, what is it?" She was frantic to know how he was hurt, but he was holding her so tightly, she couldn't even look at him. Trying to calm him, reassure him enough so that he would loosen his fierce grip, she rose on tiptoe to kiss his cheek. "It's all right," she murmured. "Con, it'll be—"

At the first touch of her lips, he turned his head in a frantic seeking until his mouth covered hers. Astonishment hit her as he lifted her into that kiss, followed by an explosion of heat flooding her womb. His hands coursed over her body as if searching for something; his tongue found hers and she made an incoherent sound.

No one had ever, ever kissed her like this, all

raw emotion, raw need, sheer passion. But she wasn't frightened, she was thrilled. Other women inspired this kind of hunger—bosomy movie stars, mysterious, exciting women who knew how to entice a man, seduce him. Things she'd never known.

Connor broke the kiss only to bury his face in the warmth of her neck and plant hot kisses there until she shivered beneath his touch. His mouth returned to hers, licking at the droplets of water, and Alix felt something, some of her own tightly bound need, breaking free. Rain pounded down, drenching them both, as his big hands cupped her bottom and he lifted her up, pressing her to the hard heat of his groin, moving her against him rhythmically.

Her fingers tangled in the wet curls at his nape before they slid downward to outline the breadth of his hard chest, his wide shoulders. He was so big, so much a man.

Touching him this way was like having a shocking fantasy come true, and having the truth be better than fantasy. His hands had slipped under her nightshirt and found the softness of her breasts. He groaned with satisfaction as he tested skin and texture. Then his fingers caught at her tight, aching nipples and she cried out.

Excitement blasted through her in shock waves she couldn't control, and her body shuddered with the power of it.

This wasn't Alix Benton, the woman in a child's body, the racetrack tomboy, or careful professional. This was someone she hadn't even known existed. Someone so overwhelmed by sheer sexual arousal that she was losing her awareness of everything, even herself.

She didn't know what had happened to make him come to her like this, but she no longer cared. She felt the rain, but didn't know she called his name at his rough caress, didn't know when he swept her nightshirt over her head and backed her against the cold, wet wall next to the glass door. She did feel the heat of his mouth as he suckled hungrily at her bare breast. Her hands caressed the wet skin of his sides and back beneath his shirt in blind, frantic motions.

She felt his hand glide down her stomach, first over, then beneath her lace panties. His long, sensitive fingers slid urgently into the warmth between her legs. Alix gasped, her knees buckling.

It was when he had to catch her slight weight that Connor suddenly realized where they were, what he was about to do.

"Alix!"

"Please," she whispered, tightening her hold as his loosened. "Don't stop!"

Something between a groan and a sigh escaped him, and he cradled her tight to his chest, lips pressed against her damp hair. There was no more thought of victims or bloody injuries, the fear in the eyes of those who loved or the indifference of a staff pushed beyond what was human. There was only this woman within his grasp, and the things she brought with her, scent and sweetness, beauty and light and warmth. And the taste of her, heaven after hell.

Above her head, his arm braced their weight against the wall. He panted gustily and threw his head back for a few moments before he bent to press his forehead to hers.

Forgive me, lassie," he whispered.

"Shhh." Her shaking fingers touched his lips. "Come inside."

She moved sideways and began to walk backward, pulling him through the open doorway. She could have left him on the couch, but bypassed it to pull him through the bedroom doorway and on into the bathroom.

Although his eyes never left her, Connor seemed dazed. By now, Alix had stopped trembling. She grabbed a short robe from the back of the door and looked up to find him staring as she tied it closed. She flipped the light on and smiled as she reached up to unbutton his shirt. Strain showed in every weary line of his face.

"Do you want to talk about it?" she asked him tentatively.

He gave a single shake of his head. "No' now."

Nodding, she pushed the soggy cotton from his shoulders. Then she gasped. She'd never seen a body like his up close. She was used to the sleek mold of hard bodies, athletes pared down to only essential bone and muscle. His was a different kind of body entirely; stronger, mightier than anything she had imagined. Every curve was wide sculpted and beautiful. His arms were covered with thick, twining muscles, and his stomach was a series of tight, rounded bands.

Her heart pounded so hard, it shook her rib cage.

"You . . . work with weights," she murmured, still staring, taking in his pale skin and dark, curling, masculine hair.

"Aye," he answered. "For the stress."

Grabbing a towel, she reached high to dry the mink dark curls that tumbled over his forehead.

He stood passive under her brisk movements, but then the motion slowed and the towel drifted to his chest. Within the terry, her hand made circles over the soft whorls of black hair and muscles there. She found his racing heartbeat. Eyes to his, she let the cloth fall and her fingers went to his belt buckle.

Alix had worried that when this moment came she would be timid or frightened or passive. She'd been wrong. There was fire and an awareness of every nerve. She was achy and impatient to touch the sleek warmth of his skin. But she only got as far as the top of his zipper before she began to tremble again.

The rasp of metal upon metal was loud in her ears, and now she couldn't help but stare at the bulge pressing the material outward. Her hands dropped.

His deep woods scent seemed to envelop them both as he reached for her, letting his thumbs slide into the vee of her thin robe. In one move, he pushed the loosely belted robe and her unruly hair back over her shoulders. Her eyes closed and her head fell back.

His hands smoothed down, shaping her sides, waist, and hips, leaving a trail of gooseflesh. His knuckles rose only long enough to graze the outsides of her small breasts. Her eyes closed tighter as she felt her nipples contract. When his thumbs tugged at the thin lace above her thighs, her last bit of clothing slid to the tile floor.

He stared down at the soft curls between her legs—sandy blond mixed with a lighter reddish color—and he let one hand cup her possessively. When she stiffened, his dark eyes met hers.

"Ye're beautiful." His voice was low and intense. In truth, he was nearly overwhelmed. Connor had never thought he had a special type of woman, but seeing the lovely sprite before him, he could think of no type more appealing to his senses . . . or his sex. Though he could see her strength of form, she was yet fragile, ethereal. Her skin was lightly tanned, still translucent, with white bikini marks he found unbearably erotic.

She shook her head, denying his words, but his mouth simply bent to hers with sweet, nibbling kisses. "I would be with ye tonight, Alixandra," he announced, his voice a low coaxing rasp. "Will ye have me?"

FOUR

Alix swallowed painfully. "Yes," she whispered.

His hand tightened for a second before it left her. Then she was raised high in his arms as he turned and made for the darkness of the bed.

The bathroom threw just enough light to show him the way, then he was lowering her to the softness of the tumbled sheets. His dark eyes glittered and changed as he pulled out his wallet and searched for a foil package. She gulped when he placed it on the night table. He pushed down his trousers, his briefs with them. So methodical, she thought. So in character.

He reached for the lamp and turned it to the softest glow while Alix let her gaze trail down his massive chest, over trim hips, to rest upon the dark hair between his legs and the rigid column of flesh that rose proudly there.

She froze. He was certainly built in proportion.

Connor smiled, studying her serious face. For a moment, she almost looked frightened. He lay down beside her and murmured, "S'bonnie." He found her mouth. "I wouldna hurt ye, lass." He felt her surrender as she sighed.

She tasted of warm honey and sweet femininity, and with each flavor, his urgency increased. He nibbled and bit at her full lips until they parted, then his tongue plunged deep, finding more heat, more sweetness. He pulled her hips closer and ground his own against them. Sweat broke out as he flushed with desire. His big, roughened hands stroked her body as he might stroke a kitten, over and over.

"Alix," he whispered hotly. "Sometimes I turn m'head and think I catch the scent of you upon the air." He bent his nose to her hair and breathed deep. Then he cupped her breast. Her breath quickened with a little gasp. His thumb circled once, twice, and finally found the luscious pink tip. "I've thought of almost nothing but you since I plucked you from the rain that day."

"Me too," she confided.

He bent and kissed her silken flesh, then his mouth found her nipple. As he began to draw upon it, she made a throaty sound and pressed his head against her. He pulled back and grinned, rubbing circles over the damp flesh with his thumb.

"Ye like that, do ye?" he teased her, looking into her bright eyes.

"It's . . . okay." She tried not to shiver as she teased back.

"That's fine, then." His hand kneaded her flesh and she shivered. "For I plan to do it more. I'd like to see ye come apart in m'arms."

As his mouth suckled her, his hand strayed over her taut stomach to lace through the soft triangle of curls. Her legs loosened with a will of their own and her hips rose in a yearning arch. Finally, his fingers parted her, finding her damp and swollen.

She cried out incoherently and Connor smiled, pleased with the way she told him what she liked.

He circled and teased, finding the sweet bud of flesh that waited. His touch shot sparks of fire, and her hands went to his shoulders. His skin was warm and smooth and seemed to vibrate under her touch. Wondering if his nipples were as sensitive as hers, she let her fingers drift lightly over them. His shudder surprised her.

So, she was not the only one affected.

All the while, Connor teased her with his fingers, one, then two, slipping deep to test the passage. God, she was hot, and tight! So tight that he would have to make sure she was very aroused or he might hurt her.

"Aye," he whispered as he pressed kisses over her cheeks and to the sensitive skin beneath her ear. "Touch me!"

She did, her hunger increasing with every caress. Finally, her good hand found the hot silk of his arousal. He stiffened and pressed her hand hard against him with his own.

"I've little control left, lassie," he said as he lifted her hand to his lips. He licked the center of her palm before he bit gently at the fleshy base of her thumb. "An' I've plans for that." He grinned, dark eyes glowing.

Then his fingers returned to the ache between her legs as he licked and bit at her nipples. When her head was turning helplessly from side to side and her hips squirming beneath him, he ran openmouthed kisses down her body. He praised her delicacy, her strength, in erotic whispers. Growling low in his throat, he took her hips in both hands. His mouth found her heat and she gave a low, helpless moan.

Heat, an inferno of heat . . . and an intimacy she had never believed existed! It was different, wildly different from anything she'd known before. She felt like kindling, and Connor's touch was the match. His tongue and mouth caressed her exquisitely, until she began to shake with great tremors and the pleasure was so rich that she was bewildered by it.

"Please, Con. Aah, please!" she moaned, the words dragged from her.

He started a knowing pattern of suction and tiny bites that sent her flying through a dazzling blackness of spiraling sensation. She cried out in a shrill voice, sobbing her surprise and pleasure.

Slowly, sweetly, he brought her down, and she felt his kiss on the inside of her thigh as her senses began to return. But tiny aftershocks shuddered through her for several minutes, and she could not speak.

When he pulled her into his arms and pushed her head onto his shoulder, she felt his hardness against her hip and touched her hand to where his heart pounded.

Both heat and tension coursed through his big body, but he seemed in no hurry. He let her catch her breath, stroking the wild jumble of her hair, the damp skin of her back and hip, then down her leg, as far as he could reach.

So giving, she thought, realizing that he could have had her and satisfied himself so easily. She was too embarrassed to tell him that she had never imagined such pleasure. A rush of warm feeling choked her. He would never know how much she had needed his generosity.

In a moment, his lips touched her temple and, without thinking, she reached up to cup one raspy cheek and pull him to her for a kiss. That kiss deepened, and she felt the groan that echoed through his great chest. His hand found her breast again, flicking her nipple while his kisses trailed along her neck, sending tremors of new arousal racing through her.

By the time she felt his touch between her legs, she was panting hard, and unashamed because she could hear his own harsh breathing. Her hips moved helplessly to his rhythm. When Connor pushed two fingers high inside her, he knew it was time.

Alix made a wordless protest at his withdrawal. But then she heard the tearing of foil and he returned. He positioned himself between her legs and reached out to drag her hips toward him.

That was the bad moment.

In a sudden flash of memory, Alix thought of the last time she had seen a man poised between her thighs in such an intimate way.

Her flesh turned cold and she stared without seeing. Then she set her chin and thrust the memory behind her. This caring man could not be compared to that. She wouldn't allow it!

Connor had seen her eyes change. Agonized, he closed his own in an effort to maintain some control of himself. God help him if she told him no. Tremors shook him like an electrical current, and he was desperate to be inside her. How would he control this?

He felt her hands on his arms, pulling him closer.

Looking straight into his eyes, Alix smiled. He groaned and hauled her to him. Hands at her thighs, his mouth devoured hers. He let his arousal test her tight heat. He was a big man and he knew it might be difficult for her to take him. His thumb found the sensitive bud above his entry and circled there as he pushed in a little farther. Her whimpers filled his mouth, then he was buried deep within her.

"Lassie?" he said hoarsely. God, he needed

to move! But she was so tight. He didn't want to hurt her.

Her hips flexed, and she arched upward with another whimper. He looked down at her flushed face and realized with rising pleasure that what he saw was impatience.

That set him free and he began to move, thrusting deep, only to withdraw almost completely. His hands cupped her firm little bottom and moved her to his need. She was hot velvet, consuming!

Alix caressed his shoulders and sides, his back. His muscles rippled beneath her fingers. She let her thumbs scrape over his dark nipples with the rhythm he set. Ecstasy shimmered through her with every move he made, and there was need; vibrating, hounding need. Sweat poured from them both, then Connor caught her close once more. In a quick move, he rolled them over until she was above him, straddling his hips. His hands cupped her breasts.

"Now ye can show me the fine rider ye are, lassie." He smiled up at her brilliantly as he rolled her nipples between his fingers.

Her head lolled to the side as she pressed down hard, feeling every inch of him within her. She couldn't believe she could contain him.

He began to use the silk of her hair, rubbing it over nipples so sensitive that her inner muscles contracted around him with every sweep.

"Sweet, bloody hell," he murmured, his hips rising beneath her.

Then she did ride him, with shifts and circling motions that drove her own need higher and higher, until she felt his hand move between her legs. Crying out, she convulsed so hard around him that seconds later Connor groaned his own release.

He wanted her again almost immediately, unable to still his hands from caressing her over and over. Reluctantly, he drew away from the sweet softness of her body, but she wouldn't let him.

"I must go to m'car, sweetheart," he whispered in her ear.

She shivered and pulled him closer. "No . . . why?"

"Because I dinna carry a dozen condoms in my wallet, ye she witch." He nipped at her breast. "And I'm sure to have need of them with the likes of ye so near."

"Doctor." She laughed huskily. "I'm scandalized."

"Nay." He smirked, giving her a quick buss. "Ye're irresistible!"

When he returned, he heard the shower and grinned as he imagined joining her there. For all her beauty, his Alix was curiously inexperienced. True, she was young, too young for him, some would say. But that would not keep him from her. He felt that he ran a path straight to her, created just for him.

Alix's eyes were full of water when the shower door opened and then closed with a rush of cool air. A second later, Connor's thumb traced the water that flowed over her spine and she gave a delicate shudder, smiling whimsically.

"Hello," she murmured, turning her head in his direction. She received a kiss where neck met shoulder.

His hands reached around and took the soap as he nibbled on an earlobe and whispered, "Hal-lo."

He proceeded to rewash every inch of her delectable body, slowly, carefully, and in great detail.

She cried out twice before he dried her and led her back to bed, where he loved her again.

* * *

"Will you tell me about it?" she asked him as they lay entwined, exhausted, his heart beating slow and steady beneath her ear. "What happened tonight?"

Moments passed, until she thought he might have fallen asleep. Then the words came out of the darkness.

"A busload of children, twelve, thirteen years old. There was an accident, then an explosion. Just children." His hoarse voice drifted off. "So many." For a moment, he couldn't speak. He rubbed his stubbled cheek against her silken hair.

"I . . . lost two tonight," he whispered. "A girl and a boy. The girl . . ." A sound escaped him. "The girl had long blond hair, but there was so much blood. It . . . her skull was fractured." His breath escaped in a rough sigh. "I couldn't save them." He tried to clear his throat, but it came out like a sob, and she gathered him more tightly to her.

"I'm sorry, Con, so sorry." His emotions filled the shadows. All she could do was hold him, giving him whatever comfort he would take. "Tell me all of it?" she asked. "Please."

And he did, in a halting voice. Finally, gratefully, he ran down.

"But so many were saved," she whispered, and held her breath until he nodded.

She lay there with him, thinking of all he'd said. She'd seen violence, too much of it at the track. Horses went down, jockeys under them. A sudden flip in the gate and you could be crushed. Sometimes a rider was forced into the rail. Boots had died that way, right before her eyes.

Alix sighed and swallowed against the pain of her memories. Eventually, she kissed Connor's hair. "I've never been responsible for another life, only my own. It seems too hard." She stroked the dark curls, wishing for the healing words. "But I know the gamble of life and death is met every day, Connor. I've seen a lot of things I'd like to forget. I know you have too. In the end, you can only do your best. You did that. You do." She pressed kisses upon his eyes, his brows and cheeks, before she found his hungry lips. "Think of the ones you saved."

He whispered her name and crushed her to him.

Alix had never slept with another human being before and lay awake long after Connor slumbered beside her. She felt safe, snuggled with him, her back to his warm front. More, she felt exultant and deliciously female.

Never again would she doubt that she could be desirable to a man. In the space of one night Connor MacLeod, with his fine, fierce passion, had erased those fears forever.

His arm lay heavy against her waist and his fingers loosely cupped one breast. Her own hand caressed his strong forearm, the silky dark hair sprinkled over satiny skin.

Even though Connor would probably remember it as a night of profound sorrow, it had been the most wonderful night of Alix's life. She didn't want it to end.

She couldn't believe how open he'd been with his feelings, how caring. He'd been tender and playful and so incredibly exciting. He'd given her the gift of pleasure, then she'd learned the depth of his compassion for others.

Dreamily, she wondered what it would be like to sleep with this great bear of a man every night, to make love with him as many times as she wanted.

She craned her neck to see the clock. It was nearly one-thirty, three hours from the time she usually got up for early workout. Disturbed at the motion, Connor pulled her back with a little snuffling snore. Her mouth quirked upward at the homey sound. She put her own hand over the big paw covering her breast. Mmm . . . he was so warm . . .

When Alix woke, it was to the feel of nuzzling kisses behind one ear. She squirmed and sighed happily. Her eyes were still closed as he turned her upon her back. She felt the rasp of his beard against her before the wet heat of his mouth closed over her nipple.

She smiled sleepily, and Connor thought he had never seen anything quite as lovely.

His hands ran over her from neck to thighs then lower, to her ankles and feet. He lifted a foot, finding her instep with his mouth, and murmured, "There are boots for feet so small and fine?"

She laughed. "I go through too many of them." Her smile deepened as his lips nibbled upward over round knees and supple thighs. She shifted beneath him.

Her arms lifted above her head and she gave a long, feline stretch before letting her eyes drift open. By that time he was back to her breast, teething the nipple with exquisite torture. She sighed. "Delicious . . ."

"True." His tongue licked her impudently.

He was about to ask if she was sore, thinking it very likely. But before he could voice the question, her hands rose to his shoulders and she surprised him with a quick shove that landed him on his back beneath her.

"I want a taste too," she said, and proceeded to explore the rich flavors of his neck, his chest, and downward. Connor responded by touching every bit of her within reach, reverently, caressingly.

When she dipped her tongue into his navel, he growled and nearly came off the bed. But she swiftly turned him over, straddling his hips for a moment before lying upon him completely. She nibbled the back of his neck and stroked down his arms.

Gooseflesh peppered his skin as she slid down farther, purring with delight at the great fists that tightened on her sheets. She kissed her way down his spine.

Her hands curved lower, over and around, and she gave his taut flesh a playful bite. She shaped the indented muscle and squeezed, fascinated. "Mmm, great buns, Doc."

No sooner did she speak, than she was bucked

aside as he twisted beneath her, throwing her upon her back again. With the next breath her legs were parted and he was inside her, warm and throbbing.

He groaned despairingly when she wrapped her legs around his. "Dinna move!"

Alix laughed with sheer joy and shifted her hips to torment him, bringing him deeper.

"Alixandra!" he commanded, and she stilled. "Dinna move. Ye got me in such a state, I forgot the condom!"

Her womb clenched with her surprise, and he groaned again. "Put yer legs down, lassie, and let me go."

"When you've got it," she said mutinously, tossing her hair over her shoulder.

"What?" He was incredulous, his scowl pulling his brows down and together.

"I'll let you go when I know you'll be right back," she said, as if to a simpleton, then she grinned. "You'll just have to take me with you."

He chuckled hoarsely. "Ye wee witch, y'll not be laughing long if I get a bairn on ye. So dinna tease."

"Where are they?" she asked impatiently.

He looked to the nightstand, miles away.

"Hurry, Connor . . ."

Their progress was a little awkward. He supported her weight with one hand on her bottom and walked on his knees across the bed. But she interspersed each step with kisses and every time she giggled, he felt her inner muscles constrict.

Sheer torture!

At last he fumbled with the package, but now Alix was the eager one. She took it away from him and opened it in one quick motion.

They both groaned when he withdrew, but those sounds soon turned to heartfelt sighs and heated passion.

When she woke again, she was alone. Still she smiled.

Connor stared at the charts on his desk without seeing them. He couldn't stop thinking about her. He'd never been out of control the way he'd been with Alix in the rain, never let his emotions run him before, not even with his wife.

But Sorcha and Alix had little in common.

Sorcha. Quiet, contained, yet she'd hated the isle with its set traditions and highland ways. She'd always wanted to go to college, but her family couldn't afford it. Connor had known her his life long, been beguiled by her flirting and her admiration. She'd been his girl since they were sixteen. Little did he know that she wanted a way off the island far more than she ever wanted him.

When she told him she was pregnant at eighteen, they did what was expected. Then Connor took the job at Cape Wrath.

He worked the offshore oil rig three weeks on, one off. It meant leaving Sorcha alone a good deal, but they'd need the money for the child. What he did not know was that Sorcha had no intentions of being tied down with a baby when she was just starting to enjoy her freedom.

Connor mourned the "miscarriage" deeply, and after that he saw his wife begin to change. She began to run with a fast crowd, drinking, spending nights in the clubs. Then came the shopping trips to Inverness and Edinburgh. After a while, he wasn't even sure if she'd be in their flat when he got there.

He didn't like her friends or her running around so much, and the arguments began. They clashed about everything and seemed to grow further and further apart. Finally, a year into the marriage, Connor's older brother, Ian, came for a visit. They were down at the pub having a pint, when the man next to them began bragging to his mates about the girl he'd had the night before for the price of a drink.

Moments later, Connor had heard enough to realize that the man was speaking of his own wife. He could see Ian knew it too. With slow deliberation, he turned and knocked the man to the ground.

When he confronted Sorcha, she laughed in his face and admitted everything. Already drunk, she blamed him for a lack of attention, for her boredom and her lovers. She despised their life, she told him, and his dull friends. She'd only stayed with him because he made good money and left her alone. Then she told him about the abortion.

Numbness permeated every fiber of his being. For a long moment, he stared into her hate-filled eyes and wondered how she'd hidden her feelings so well. One lie after another. And he had planned to build a life with her! He'd never felt such a fool.

He turned and left her then.

After Ian nursed him through a week-long drunk in Edinburgh, Connor took a good look at his life and determined to change it. And he wanted to be as far away from Cape Wrath as he could get.

He'd been divorced for years now, but he still remembered those feelings, the shame of having been so blind, the agony of betrayal. Somehow, Alixandra Benton had slipped past his defenses as if they were so much warm butter . . . and left him eager for more.

Pictures of the night before had tantalized him all through the day, in the midst of procedures, while he read charts. In his mind he kept seeing her astride him, face flushed, mouth open slightly as she made soft pleasure cries. The wildflower scent of her was in his head, woven now with erotic memories, and that morning he'd even called Muñiz by Alix's name.

It wasn't like him.

FIVE

Santa Anita. It made her heart pound just to be on the grounds. The smells of fresh hay and horses, the sounds of hooves and harnesses combined to make her nerves sizzle and adrenaline sail through her bloodstream.

The racetrack was beautiful in any season, a California painting with the oriental sculpture of its olive trees and deco landscaping of yellow and blue-violet pansies. The San Gabriel mountain range created a perfect snow-tipped frame.

Alix might like the track best at sunrise with an eager mount under her, but she was delighted to share its splendor with Connor now.

He had forgone his usual suit for a fawn-colored suede jacket and cream shirt with a darker tie. The smell of suede and man teased her senses. She grinned, thinking that her cropped eyelet shirt and jeans made them a distinctively unusual couple.

"Hundreds of sea gulls live here," she said, watching the birds fly past to land upon the track. "It's so far from the ocean, no one really knows how they first came here or why. Now they live on what the crowds leave. But they're here, and they're beautiful. Three or four times a day they sweep down from the roof and over the track, as if in blessing. We love them.

"This is called the 'backside' or 'backstretch,' " she went on, hooking an arm through the one he offered as they walked down the dirt track to the guard's hut. "It really just means the stables and hot-walking area." She gave a comic sniff. "See?"

Connor's normal expression was lightened today. She was glad he had asked to see what it was like to work at the track. He even let one side of his mouth quirk at her childish humor.

Looking up at him, she thought again how lucky she was just to be with him—for however short a time. He was a gorgeous man, sleek and powerful. Better yet, he treated her with a tender care she had learned not to expect from anyone. And, she thought with a flash of wicked memory, he made her feel very, very womanly.

"Hey, Hap." She smiled at the portly guard as she signed them in. "How you doin' today?"

"Fine, Alix. You lookin' real good. How's the hand?"

"Be riding in a week or so," she answered as she took Connor's visitor tag. "Back here," she said to Connor as she stuck the tag to his chest with a tiny caress, "gossip is air to breathe. The true and the untrue. What people don't know backside just isn't worth knowing."

There were horses everywhere, led by handlers, ponygirls or boys. They were on their way back or forth from their morning workout. Grooms leaned on hay bales sipping coffee, while dogs wandered in and out of the shade. A gray-bearded goat sat high on a pile of old straw and surveyed his surroundings.

"That's Solomon," Alix said, "and that's his pile." She giggled. "He was named after *King Solomon's Mines.* As in, 'This pile is mine!' "

He harrumphed, but she knew it was a laugh.

Backside was a close-knit, friendly world. They were greeted by smiles and jokes from everyone. Connor couldn't exactly put his finger on why, but he felt the very air crackle with excitement.

They got close to a stable painted hunter-green and white, with flowers everywhere. "Wallingham's barn," Alix said, smiling. "Nothing but good stuff comes out of here. Come on, I'll introduce you to a couple of the kiddies." Then she warned him. "Stay in the center, right behind me and away from the stalls. These are all thoroughbreds. They're big, and they're primed, ready to race." She grinned up at him. "They'd like nothing better than to take a nice bite of you to let off some steam. And if you hear something behind you, move fast. Horses have the right of way here . . . and they can kick hard."

"I have no intent of even leaving your side," he said warily, but he looked completely at ease.

They walked through quickly, Alix showing off a few of her favorite rides. Connor watched the way she was with the beasts, confident but gentle, as she rubbed a velvet muzzle or a satin neck.

"This is Pride of Place." She beckoned Connor closer to a stall. "He's the gelding I was riding the day I broke my hand." She held the bridle with her good left hand and took one of Connor's big hands in her right, lifting it high on Pride's dark nose. "He's got a sweet spot, right . . . here." She guided his fingers over the small white star between the gelding's eyes. The big thoroughbred snuffled happily.

Time seemed to slow as they caressed Pride together. Connor's thumb slid over hers.

"Boots always told me to watch a man's hands, that you could trust a man with gentle hands," Alix said in a hushed voice. "A horse can feel the difference in one touch." She looked up into his long-lashed eyes. They drew her again and again. "Maybe . . . like I did when you touched me. You have the most gentle hands of anyone I've ever known."

His breath dragged in, and Connor pulled his hand away from her to stuff it in his pants pocket. "Get me out of here, lassie, afore I put one of these stalls to the use I'm thinkin' of."

She kept looking at him and smiled sweetly, the look in her aquamarine eyes warm and open . . . and sexy. He knew there was no way out, no way to save himself.

He bent and kissed her. Slow and warm, the kiss went on and on. He lifted her up and into him, until they heard someone coming into the stable.

They stumbled outside, and Alix shielded her eyes from the bright morning light as she regained her composure. Glancing toward the track, she saw a small crowd gathered there, between the stands and the first stables.

"That's where we'll find Sammy," she said. "He'll be checking the horses, looking them over for the winners. Then he'll work their trainers, talking them into putting his jockeys up on them." She spotted his tweed-checkered jacket with the condition book sticking out of the pocket before she saw his balding head. Sammy always wore a checkered jacket.

Smiling fondly, she pointed out the wiry little man to Connor. "There he is. Come on, I want to introduce you. Being an agent is very competitive. Sammy's great."

"Hey, doll!" Sammy greeted her with a wide, buck-toothed smile. "Lemme see you!" He peered into her face, his beetle brows rising, then glanced at the man beside her. "Hmm. Lemme see that hand."

She suffered his examination and grinned when he muttered, "Those quacks better've done a good job on you. These hands are our fortune."

Connor lifted an eyebrow and stood a little taller, towering over them both as Alix said, "Sammy, there's someone I'd like you to meet."

"Yeah?" He squinted up at the tall, dark Scot.

"This is Connor MacLeod." She could barely hold back her laughter. They looked like a rooster and a chick facing off. "My doctor." She blushed rose-red and finished, "And friend."

"Hmm," Sammy said again, taking in the size of the man, his clothes.

"Very nice to meet you." Connor held out a hand. Sammy shook it, if somewhat cautiously.

"Sammy," Alix said quickly, "I want to make a run to the stewards' office. Can I leave Connor with you for a minute? Maybe you can explain some of what goes on out there."

Sammy's head bobbed once. "Sure thing." He pulled out a cigar, lit it, and took Connor's measure once again. "Ain't never met any men *friends* of Alix before. Come on," he said, motioning Connor forward to the rail. "Come on over here. I'll show you the competition."

"Mine or hers?" Connor asked.

That earned him a grin as Sammy looked up a foot or so at him. "Strictly business, tall man. Strictly kosher business."

The stewards confirmed that no other information had come to light regarding the barbed-wire incident. Although most racing people were dedicated animal lovers and would never hurt a horse, there were many low-paying jobs on the track and always someone who would do anything for a buck.

Alix was headed back, passing one of the hot-walking rings, when she saw Dani ahead of her. Alix watched her for a minute, admiring her seat, her grace. High on her mare, Dani was leading a gelding back from the track when she caught sight of Alix. She waved and beckoned. Alix grinned back. She couldn't wait to see her cocky friend's face when she got her first look at Connor.

Suddenly, Dani's wave changed and she was standing up in the irons, yelling something. Alix felt the hair rise at the back of her neck as she swung around, just in time to see a loose horse the size of a Mack truck bearing down on her. With a one-step twist to the right, she leapt into a stack of hay bales, protecting her cast as she rolled as far from those flashing hooves as she could get.

The next thing Alix knew, Dani was patting her down, cussing up a storm as she rattled off a series of questions in Spanish to the stallion's shamefaced groom. His answers were long and incomprehensible to Alix.

"Damn greenhorns!" Dani continued patting, ignoring Alix's protests that she was fine.

"Will you let me up!" Alix finally managed to push Dani away and get to her feet.

Dani was still sputtering. "I can't believe Dunhill would let a stableboy this green get near a wild card like Best Bandit!"

"It happens all the time, Dani, and you know it. It's just a question of bad luck. Horses are always getting loose back here, even if the handler's experienced." Alix didn't want to think about other possibilities. It would only be paranoia.

But Dani was having none of it. She jammed her fists into her hips. "Alix, this guy has been mucking stalls for a week, that's it! He says the Horse Identifier told him to bring Bandit out of the stall for a picture, and he did it because it was a track official." She frowned and her voice hardened. "But he said it was a *man*, Alix! That the man deliberately frightened the horse. All other doubts aside, Diane and Sandy are the only IDers here and they are both, quite obviously, women. Another thing, Bandit's been running this track all season. They have to have his picture on file already."

Alix paled. "Maybe something happened to the file copy." She and Dani exchanged looks that said neither of them believed that.

Dani shrugged and said, "Let's just have a run over to the receiving barn and ask 'em." Alix pursed her lips, nodding solemnly.

Diane and Sandy knew nothing about it. Better yet, they flatly denied there being another IDer on the track. Official calls were made to the gate and to the stewards. It would be much more difficult for stray types to get backside after this incident.

"What's going on, Alix?" Dani demanded as soon as they were on the path outside. "Why are these things happening?"

"Nothing's going on, Dani. Well," she added with a quick grin, "there is . . . something going on . . . but not with barbed wire or loose horses."

"Say what?" Dani exclaimed, hands on her small hips.

"Come on and see." Alix laughed out of sheer happiness as she dragged Dani to the gap, where Connor and Sammy stood at the rail. "Don't say anything about Bandit. Sammy was so bent out of shape about the wire, I don't want him imagining things."

Dani gave her a black look, but her silence was agreement.

When they got closer, Alix was happy to see Connor paying rapt attention while Sammy gestured to one galloping horse, then another.

Dani caught sight of Connor and turned a wink on Alix. "Will you look at that 'hunk o' hunk o' burnin' love'!"

Alix laughed. "My thoughts exactly!"

They were no more in Alix's door than Connor backed her against one wall of her foyer for a kiss that bordered on voracious.

All the way home from the track, he'd tortured himself with images of what he was going to do to her when he got her alone. Now he planned to do every one of them.

His lips played over hers, pursuing her taste, her sweetness, that warm, honest response. Nipping, shaping her mouth, he growled with relief at the feel of her in his arms.

Alix had longed for him all day, and his hunger inspired hers. Eager little murmurs slipped from her while she reached frantically for his tie and dragged the knot loose. Then she was tearing at his shirt, lifting one knee high so that she could get closer to that hard heat she needed.

"You feel so good," she said between kisses as she pushed jacket and shirt away.

"Aye," he agreed. His hands were everywhere, roving her back, her sides and waist. "But I never meant to use ye s'harshly."

"What do you mean?" she asked, puzzled.

"Are ye not a wee bit tender, lassie?" he asked in his sure, straightforward manner.

A blush burned her cheeks, and she tried to pull away.

" 'Tis only natural." He tried to soothe her.

When she squirmed again in his arms, he held her tighter.

"Ye know me as a doctor, Alix. Did ye believe I wouldna care if I hurt ye?" His eyes were dark, unreadable.

"You didn't hurt me," she countered.

"An' I have na wish to," he said, and picked her up. A dear habit, she thought. He brought her to the bed, where he laid her gently down. "I've just the thing."

"Honey!" She watched suspiciously as he set the little plastic bear on the bed table beside a bowl of ice water. "What is this, some kind of Scottish folk medicine?"

He ignored her until he came back from the

bathroom with a washcloth. "Dinna scoff at what you dinna ken," he answered loftily. He proceeded to remove her clothing, piece by piece. "These blue jeans are a scandal," he murmured as he slid the zipper down and dipped two fingers between her thighs with a sly wiggle. "They make a man think of naught but getting them from ye." He rubbed the thin material of her panties against her until her hips rose, then he withdrew to pull the denim to her feet. Sliding downward, he drew in a deep breath and closed his eyes in ecstasy at the scent of her. Then he smiled, and Alix had never seen anything so erotic in her life.

When they were both naked, with only the afternoon light caressing their skin, Connor sat on the side of the bed and dipped the washcloth in the ice water. Alix's eyes widened and she rose on one elbow.

Connor smiled tolerantly, mysteriously. "Lie down."

She looked at him a minute as he half wrung the cloth. He seemed strangely uncivilized without his tie and other gentlemanly trappings. She wanted to run her fingers over his chest and down his corded belly. One hand couldn't resist reaching out to caress the thick, ruddy shaft. He moved in her hand and gave her a look that would have melted steel. "Lie down," he said again.

Her tongue came out to moisten dry lips, and she thought he'd change his mind. But his eyes were steady on hers until she did as he asked.

"First cold," Connor explained, trying to keep his breath even, regular, "then heat." Her eyelids grew heavy, and he knew his grin belied his dispassionate instruction. "It's the time-proven method of reducing edema, or swelling." He put a couple of cubes in the center of the cloth and closed it, then turned to her. Placing the cloth just above her breast, he let a droplet of water fall to glaze her nipple. She gasped.

"The cold," he continued, moving the cloth so that it brushed the hardened bud, "makes the tissue contract." Concentrating upon his task, Connor paid the same attentions to her other breast, then dragged the cloth lightly down the center of her body, circling her navel, and down over the mound of her femininity. Ignoring her quickened breathing, he said, "Part your legs for me, Alix."

She shook her head. "Too cold."

"I'll take care o' you, lassie." He looked deep into her fairy eyes.

Finally, reluctantly, she let her legs slide apart for him. The first touch of the icy cloth against her hot flesh made her hips jerk in panic.

"Whisht, lassie," he whispered as he bent to sip at a nipple. "Easy."

He stroked her lightly, lightly, until she longed for pressure. He began to follow each stroke of the cold cloth with one of his callused thumb over the same flesh. She gasped again as she felt two fingers slide into her hot sheath. They moved carefully, and she moaned when she felt them withdraw. Her eyes flew open when she realized a melting ice cube had replaced them.

"What . . . ?" she cried.

"Shhh, just here," he reassured her, "where ye're swollen."

He cooled her and teased her for what seemed like an eternity, until her legs had parted even farther and her hips rose and fell with each motion of the cloth. Then, eyes burning black with desire, he put the cloth back in the bowl and reached for the honey.

"I think we're ready for the heat principle," he said as he touched a finger to the cone-shaped top of the bear and tasted the honey. He squeezed another drop on his finger and placed it against her lips.

Her eyes never left his as she licked and then bit his finger, drawing it deep into her mouth. He made a low sound and removed it slowly.

Smiling, he turned the bear upside down and made languid, dripping designs over her torso. "Lie still."

Alix watched each drop fall in slowest motion to pool upon her skin. She was so sensitized now, she squirmed even at the delicate weight of the honey. Then Connor was between her legs, holding her bent knees apart as he coated her succulent pink flesh.

"So much?" she breathed.

"Mmm," he answered. "You're right." He drew her legs closed and splayed his hands over her thighs. "You'll have to hold it for me until I can get to it. We Scots are a thrifty lot." His grin was wicked. "I wouldna wish to waste any."

The thick gold liquid warmed against her, and she shivered at the luxurious sensation. She opened her eyes to find Connor watching her as he touched a honey-covered nipple, then placed his finger to his tongue.

"So sweet." His voice was a low rumble. "Taste," he ordered before he leaned down to kiss her.

Slow and deep, he loved her mouth as he would soon love her body. Her fingers splayed against his scalp and held him there while she rubbed her tongue against his, moving her mouth with his, nipping at his lower lip in more and more desperate motions.

He pulled away to lap at her breasts, one after the other. She watched as his tongue laved them, flicking at the rosy nipples. She sighed deeply when he finally drew upon her with heated suction. Her legs had begun to part as he reached her navel, but he quickly straddled her, holding them closed with his thighs.

He gave her navel particular attention, letting his sipping kisses follow each design he had made with the honey. When he let her legs open for him at last, Alix sighed.

Smiling with heated anticipation, he parted her legs wide and looked down. A shudder traced his spine and ended in his groin, swelling his arousal to painful proportions as his eyes traced the glistening rose-colored folds.

His hands caressed her hips and curved down to squeeze her soft buttocks. The honey warmed all over again. In one motion, he lifted her to his hot mouth. Just before he kissed her he promised, "I'll make ye fly, lassie."

Then she was burning with his fire. The suction alternated with circling motions as he tasted, driving her faster and higher. Only seconds passed before she called his name, her body quivering with pleasure. But he didn't stop. His tongue simply moved lower, darting in and out, and it all began again.

It was midafternoon when the doorbell rang. Alix was still in the shower, so Connor traded the sheet for his pants and went to answer it, snagging his shirt along the way.

What he found when he opened the door was a box of bloodred roses and a delivery man built like a wrestler, who looked as surprised as he was.

"Flowers," the man grunted. He ducked his head and touched the bill of his baseball cap. "Flowers for Alixandra Barstow."

Connor looked him over before he corrected, "Benton."

The man ducked his head again. "Right." He thrust the box at Connor and turned away. Connor frowned. The man hadn't even waited for a tip. His frown deepened as he carried the open box back to the bedroom.

Alix came out of the bathroom dressed in a thick white terry robe, ruffling her hair with a towel. Her smile turned from angelic to brilliant when she saw what he held in his arms.

"Oh, Connor. How in the world did you—"

He cut her off. "I didn't. These must be from another of your admirers." She looked surprised, and his scowl was grim. "Why do you not read the card, lass?"

He couldn't doubt the puzzlement on her face. But when she took the box and placed it on the bed, she found no card.

"There must be some kind of mistake," she said at last. "What was the name of the florist?"

"I saw no name . . . and the man had nothing for me to sign. Neither did he wait for a tip." He fingered a plump red bloom. "Perhaps it was a mistake. The name he gave was Alixandra Barstow."

"Wh-what did you say?" She dropped to the edge of the bed, her legs unable to hold her. "Who was it he asked for?"

"Alixandra Barstow." Connor's blood was churning, and he looked at her as if for the first time. She looked small and somehow vulnerable. But she knew that name, Barstow. He saw it on her face. "When I told him it was Benton, he agreed fast enough." He waited for her to explain, but she said nothing. "'Tis certain ye know naught of it?"

That made her indignant. Her eyes shot fire to his. "I don't lie, Connor."

"That's fine," he answered, his face set in stone, his heart still pounding. "For if there's one thing I canna abide, 'tis a liar."

Outside, the man in the baseball cap slid into the waiting van. "What?" the blond man in the front seat demanded. "Why aren't you in there, dammit!"

"She's not alone," the wrestler type answered flatly. "You paid me for one job, not two. Besides, I'd need hardware to take that guy out. It won't look like an accident."

"She has a man in there?" The idea infuriated him. He'd checked the place quite thoroughly. Hers was the only car in the drive. It was a quiet Monday afternoon and the neighbors were at work. It was perfect. Perfect! Instead, the little bitch made him wait while she pleasured herself with some stud!

Bentley began to tremble with temper and tried to slow his breathing. "Let's go," he said in a voice like cold steel. "We can wait. He can't be with her all the time."

The dream came that night.

It was her birthday and Maud had spent weeks planning the party. She had invited a host of proper young ladies and gentlemen Alix had never met. Arrangements had been made for a band, a society columnist, and even a proper dress.

Alix found the dress on the pink coverlet of her bed. At first glance, she thought her aunt had done it to begin another battle. It was like too many dresses Maud had tried to force upon her through the years. It was like Maud and nothing like Alix; feminine, sweet, purest white.

A dress for a princess, it had puffed sleeves and a full skirt that rustled like whispers in the dark.

Alix touched the neckline, a fold in the skirt, and turned away. Most girls her age would look beautiful in a dress like that. But even at fifteen, Alix was still reed thin and gawky as a newborn foal. She sighed, knowing she would look ridiculous. The dress was everything she was not. Two steps from the bed, she turned back.

Maybe she was wrong. Maybe a dress like

that could somehow change her. She picked up the hem and bit her lip. For once, she wanted to know what it felt like to be alluring, feminine.

And she did feel those things when she descended the long curving staircase in her two-and-a-half-inch white pumps. When she danced with the "nice young men" who had surrounded her, she felt shy, yet powerful. Even her aunt smiled benignly at her. It was a lovely party.

She never saw Bentley watching her, watching the happiness transform her. She didn't see the look in his eyes as he listened to his mother boasting about Alix's accomplishments in school. Since he'd just been suspended from Andover, that galled him more than anything.

Unaware of the dark side that drove her cousin, Alix never imagined he would follow her out to the gazebo after the party.

She had come out to be alone. Filled with elation and pleasure of the night, she leaned back against one of the support posts. She brushed proudly at the white taffeta skirt of her gown and gazed at the stars. Hearing a creak of wood behind her, she began to turn toward the sound. Suddenly she was shoved around and pressed back against the post.

Fear choked her for an instant. Then she realized it was just Bentley.

"Oh, it's you," she said, annoyed that he had scared her.

"That's right, little cat." He leaned closer, smelling of stale liquor, and she didn't like the look in his eye. "It's me."

Her heart began a pounding beat. His voice sounded so strange.

"Fifteen. All grown up, aren't we?" His hand came between them and gave her breast a painful squeeze.

"Don't, Bentley!" Shocked, she tried to squirm away, but his hold was too tight. He quickly gathered her wrists in one hand and pressed his forearm against her windpipe. She couldn't breathe. She struggled, but he was much bigger and a great deal stronger than she.

"So grown up and so big for her britches," he spat out. "Well, let's see just how much a woman you are." With those words, he used his free hand to tear at the bodice of her dress. The ripping sound was loud in her ears. Then she was flying through the air as he jerked her away from the post. She landed faceup on the hardwood floor with a thud that sent the breath rushing from her lungs.

What was wrong with him? Why was he doing this to her?

Then he was on her again. She tried to claw his face, but he captured her hands and held them above her with one of his. Straddling her, he ripped the rest of her bodice away.

"Ha!" He laughed derisively. "You still got the body of a boy, don't you, Cat?" He gave a sharp, hurtful twist to her small nipple.

She hardly registered the pain, she was so shocked and frightened. For a moment, she had no voice. Then she began to scream until she felt a sledgehammer jolt to her jaw. In her mind, the scream continued.

SIX

Connor woke to the feel of Alix struggling in his arms. She was whimpering, "No—no!" Over and over she cried out, her arms flailing against him.

"Alix," he said groggily, but she didn't wake. He captured her hands and held them to the sides of her head, careful of her cast. "Alix, wake up! Ye're dreaming!"

Her eyes flew open. Still struggling, she was panting with fear, her body covered with sweat.

"It's all right." Connor gathered her to his chest, feeling wildly possessive as he pushed the tangled disorder of her hair away from her damp face. He cupped her cheeks in his hands and whispered again, "It's all right, sweetheart."

At the sound of that endearment, she blinked and swallowed until she could speak. "Connor . . . I—I'm sorry."

"Sorry?" He frowned down at her in the darkness. "Lass, ye had a bad dream, a nightmare. Ye ken?"

"Yes, I . . ." She shivered, and he drew her head down to his shoulder.

"Give ye'rself a moment to calm," he said as he stroked her hair. "That dream, it frightened ye." He kissed the top of her head and continued to caress her until he felt her heart beat more normally against him.

"D'ye remember what frightened ye so?" he asked after a time, his hand still upon her hair.

Alix shook her head quickly and buried her face against him, drawing in his warm scent. She didn't want to think about it. "Monster," she mumbled.

His arms tightened around her. "Ye're safe here, sweetheart. No monsters. Tell me. It will help chase the thing from you."

"No!" She jerked out of his arms and stumbled toward the bathroom. She closed the door tight behind her and turned. Facing herself in the mirror wasn't easy. She knew what she would find in her eyes.

Terror.

Her hair was a matted tangle over one shoulder, and beads of perspiration still dotted her brow and upper lip. Her nostrils flared. She could smell it on her body, the fear.

It wasn't fair to him. Connor had no way of knowing what a basket case she really was.

She turned the shower on and stepped under the hot spray, letting it cover and comfort her. Her head rolled back and she felt her tears mingle with the shower's blast as the last edges of her panic dissipated.

Draped in a towel, she finally left the bathroom. She hesitated at the sight of Connor sitting on the edge of the bed, his knees spread, hands clasped between them. He raised his head and looked at her.

"How d'ye feel, sweetheart?"

She took three steps and sank to her knees before him. "Happy you're here," she said, resting her palms on his bare thighs.

He smiled and hooked two fingers in the place between her breasts where the towel was tucked. "Good," he said before he tugged and the damp material fell away.

"I like it when you call me that," she said shyly, arching her back.

Her words rocked something in him, and he hardened instantly. He lifted her to the bed and rolled over until he lay above her.

"I'm that glad, sweetheart," he murmured as his mouth found hers.

A week went by, a miracle of a week. Alix started cooking enormous meals for the pleasure of watching Connor eat. She even learned to get used to the many small courtesies he performed. Sometimes he brought her flowers or cookies, sometimes he just appeared at her door with a look of such heat in his eyes, she thought she would melt into a puddle at his feet.

And he made her breathless with anticipation, wondering where and how he would take her next. The man had an appetite for sex that surpassed even his appetite for food. Alix found she had an appetite too—for him, anywhere, anytime he wanted.

He took her to his favorite Italian restaurant, where the chef made a great fuss over them. Then they drove to the beach and walked along the sand in the moonlight. The sea smelled glorious, like an evening promise, and the spray danced in the air like a cool whirlwind.

Alix felt happier than she could ever remember as she stole a sidelong glance at the man beside her. He looked so appealing with his impeccable pants rolled up to his knees, his strong calves bare. She wore his jacket around her shoulders, and he carried both pairs of shoes. She took his hand and smiled fondly. He looked more carefree than she had ever seen him.

"You'll be riding again soon," he said as they walked.

She watched his toes dig into the wet sand. "Yup," she answered cheerfully.

In a flash, the frown was back in its usual place. " 'Tis a verra dangerous occupation, Alixandra."

"You gonna worry 'bout me, big guy?" The thought warmed her, awed her.

He stopped walking and looked out to sea. "Aye," he said slowly.

Her other hand reached out to cover his. "I'm really very good, you know."

"So your Sammy has told me." His sensual mouth twisted slightly. He ran the ER closest to the track; he knew how often a jockey took a fall.

"I wish you could feel what it's like, Connor," she whispered as she leaned into him. "To be so high, to be one with an animal of such heart and grace and speed that it's truly like flying."

His arm came around her. "It means a great

deal to you. So that ye wouldna think of doing anything else?"

"Maybe one day, when my reputation is so strong, I can walk into a job as a trainer with the big owners. But that's a lot of wins away yet."

He stared down at her. "And a family, Alix, have you thought about that in your future?"

She laughed and smiled dreamily. "Riding's really not as dangerous as it looks from your side of the fence. If I ever got pregnant"—she paused, thinking about chocolate-eyed children— "I would just take off until after the baby was born. I make enough money. Boots and I used to talk about it, though I never really took the idea too seriously." Her throat began to close. It was stupid to think of planning a future when she didn't know how long her one and only relationship might last. "But I don't think I'm ready for that yet. It was incredibly hard to break into this field of high-money jocks. I feel like I just got here."

He pulled her closer, arms over her shoulders. She smiled, hers snaking around his waist.

"And if ye had to choose?" he asked urgently, his lips in her hair.

She thought about it, wondering if that day would ever come. Squaring her shoulders, she looked up at the stars.

"Would someone who truly cared for me force me to choose?" she asked.

The next day was Tuesday, the second day of the racetrack "weekend." Dani and Alix had made plans to work out at eight. How was Alix to have anticipated her workout would happen much earlier, and without her even having to leave the bedroom?

She never slept past five, even when she wasn't riding that day. But when she heard the doorbell Tuesday morning, she just turned into her pillow with an agonized groan.

That groan was followed by a low "Mmm" near her ear that made her smile. She had to get up and answer the door . . . had to do it . . .

Connor propped himself on an elbow as he looked down at Alix's loosely sprawled limbs. Well, it seemed he was in for another mystery visitor.

He grabbed his pants and headed for the door, bare chested. When he swung it open, he wasn't prepared for the five-foot friend of Alix's who had stared at him at the track the week before with open mouth, wild glances, and unasked questions.

"Wow!" she exclaimed, adjusting her baseball cap as she stared at his torso in sheer delight. "Great pecs!" Dani popped her gum and stepped past him.

Slightly bemused, Connor could only stare after her as the girl marched right to the bedroom door and disappeared inside. Grinning, he followed.

Inside the bedroom, he found Dani sitting on the side of the bed. Alix was propped up against the headboard, rosy red and clutching the sheet to her breasts.

"I—I slept in," she stammered to Connor. "Dani and I were supposed to work out this morning."

"Yeah," Dani said as she turned to smirk at him. "And am I shocked!" She stared pointedly at the black briefs lying on the floor. "I think you done tuckered her out, Doc."

"Naught that a hot shower shouldn't cure." His eyes focused on Alix's with a secret message before he reached for his shirt.

"Why do ye not come into the kitchen, Dani? I think I could be persuaded to give ye a cup of coffee, even breakfast if ye're good."

At the kitchen table, Dani munched on fruit and watched in awe as Connor packed away a huge omelet with four pieces of toast and sliced tomatoes.

"How come you're here on a Tuesday?" she asked. "I thought you were some big honcho doctor or something."

"I set my own schedule." He got up to pour himself more coffee. "It's one of the advantages of being a partner."

Dani made a mocking noise to show that she was impressed. "So, you serious with Alix or, uh, you just foolin' around?" she asked with her usual insouciance. Connor watched her steadily over his cup of coffee until she blushed. "I'm a friend, okay? I just don't want to see her get hurt."

"I think, perhaps, it would be best if you let the two of us muddle through on our own," he reprimanded her lightly.

"We'll see," Dani returned, a warning in the lift of her eyebrows that made him smile.

When Alix joined them, Connor served her a minuscule version of his omelet, and Dani shrugged.

"Well, if we're not going to work out I want to ask a favor." Dani munched an apple, and Alix looked up inquiringly. "I was going to wait and ask when you were too tired to refuse. Can I borrow the Alfa?"

"My car, my baby?" Alix let her eyes narrow. "What's up, Dani?"

"I want to run down to the Warner Farm for an interview. My beater might make it and it might not." She looked up at Alix with soft doe eyes. "It could be all the work I need at Hollywood Park, and maybe I can start to apprentice at Del Mar. What do you think? You got the hunk here and you said he won't take your cast off till tomorrow anyway. So you can't drive, right?"

Alix saw the amusement in Connor's eyes at being labeled a hunk.

"You hurt that car, you die." She pointed her finger at Dani.

"Hey, didn't you teach me all I know about riding? Would I do anything to alienate a free tutor?" Dani crunched another bite of the apple. "Aww." She grimaced at the window. "It's starting to rain again. Can I steal a raincoat?"

"Sure." Alix gave her a deadpan stare. "Take my car, my things. Feel free." She grinned as Connor excused himself to clear the table. "Just leave the big Scot."

"Who would'a thought it?" Dani made a silly face while she unwrapped a piece of gum and popped it in her mouth. "Bambi and the Beast!" She gave Alix a sly look. "He is a beast, I hope?"

"Get outta here, brat!" Alix was trying not to laugh. Dani snickered all the way to the front door. Turning, she waggled her fingers playfully at Connor through the open kitchen door. "You kids be go—I mean, have fu—Mmm, maybe I just better wish you safe sex, huh?" Her gum popped as she snagged a poncho from the closet by the door. She pulled it on over her head, leaving the hood up, and called, "Bye, y'all!"

Alix heard the slam of the door and turned back to Connor. He was standing next to her, pouring more coffee into her cup.

"So," she said as she lifted a bold hand and traced the warm bulge between his legs. It was just below her eye level. "All this extra free time and no idea what to do with it." He had hardened at the first brush of her hand and now his arousal strained against the twill trousers.

She glanced up at him as she lowered his zipper in careful motions. She remembered that his briefs lay on her bedroom floor. The coffee-pot was lowered to the table with a clack of glass against wood. His hands cupped her face, and he smiled down at her, hunger lighting his eyes.

"What are ye doing, ye wee mischief?"

"Exploring," she said, and flicked the button open. She saw his wide chest move as his breathing quickened. Then she was holding him in her hands, concentrating on the shape and feel of him. His fingers threaded into her hair and he groaned. When he felt her hot, moist breath, his hands tightened and he gave a start. But it was too late. It was much too late to stop.

Outside, a dark sedan followed the little red car as it left the garage and wound down the hillside road. The first time it grazed her rear bumper, Dani chewed fast and thought the guy was just a jerk who didn't know how to drive in the rain. She turned the windshield wipers higher and tried to see him through the rivulets pouring over the back window. By the third time he bumped her, she decided she had a maniac on her tail.

Her work with horses saved her life. Dani was used to the unpredictability of animals in the rain, so her reflexes were sharp. They rounded a corner and the sedan pulled into the oncoming lane, smashing into the side of the Alfa-Romeo with a loud crunching sound and forcing Dani into the brush.

Knowing that where brush ended, the steep slope of the hill began, Dani felt her heart in her throat as she hauled the wheel back to the left, colliding with the right fender of the sedan.

The driver of the sedan slammed on his brakes and wrenched the wheel to the right, forcing the Alfa off the road, down the hill, in a rocking roller coaster ride that ended when Dani slammed into a boulder.

The sedan pulled to the right shoulder, and a big man got out, looking for the Alfa. He started down the hill, when he saw a black-and-white police car coming toward him. From inside the car, a voice issued a harsh command and he obeyed, leaping back into the car and flooring the accelerator.

The cop in the black-and-white gave a narrow-eyed look and started to make a U-turn, but then he saw the fragments of red taillight glass and thick black skid marks going off the rain-washed road.

Alix and Connor were lying entwined on the living room rug when the call came from Dani's sister.

Connor had never seen Alix look like this before. Her eyes seemed twice their normal size while her cheeks were pale and drawn. Her bottom lip was swollen where she had bitten it over and over on the drive to the hospital. There, she pushed open the door to Dani's room with a stealth brought forth by dread.

Dani was a slight figure in the white-sheeted bed with a bandage over her nose. She had a tube in one arm, and her eyes were closed. Purple bruises lay beneath both eyes.

"Dani," Alix whispered. "Dani honey?"

Dani's dark lashes fluttered. "Alix?"

Tears filled Alix's eyes, but she blinked them away. "How you feelin', brat?"

Dani gave a halfhearted smile and said, "Scared of you."

"What do you mean?" Alix asked, a hurt expression on her face.

"I wrecked your baby, didn't I?"

"Didn't I mention I needed a new paint job?" Alix said, and received a watery chuckle in return.

"What happened, brat?" Alix asked, and Dani told them. They talked for a few more minutes about her free nose job until Dani seemed to tire. Connor stood behind Alix, doing no more than squeezing Dani's hand. But he was a warm presence for both of them.

* * *

Alix was preoccupied during the next few days. Nervous too. Connor had finally taken off the cast and pronounced her fit to ride, but she was taking it slow. She worked four or five horses every morning to get the muscle tone back in her injured hand, but it would be a few more days before she wanted a race.

Still, it felt good to be back.

She was riding from the gap onto the track when she happened to glance over to the crowd who'd come to watch the early workout. That's when she saw him. It was a face Alix still saw in her nightmares, one she couldn't forget.

Reflexively, she jerked the reins, causing her mount to rear in protest until the pony-boy helped get him under control. Her heart thudding in her ears, Alix stared back over her shoulder, searching the crowd. But the face was gone.

Connor had just finished a leg dressing when Muñiz put her hand on his arm. "Connor?"

He looked up, startled. Muñiz never called him by his first name. Her gaze moved to the white curtain and his followed. His heart began to slam as he straightened and looked from the nurse's face to the curtain and back again. Time and motion seemed to slow as he walked to the curtain and pushed it back.

It was Alixandra. Eyes closed, she lay still, unmoving. Her head had a bloody cut that would take two sutures, and she had a backboard strapped to her neck to stabilize it.

Using all his discipline to stay calm, he checked her pupils, her ears for bleeding. His panic would do her no good. Her pupils responded to the light, and he found no bleeding from ears or mouth.

"Vital signs?" he demanded sharply.

"Good vitals," Muñiz announced with her usual efficiency. "BP's one hundred and twenty over ninety, pulse sixty-five, respiration's twenty, temp ninety-eight point seven."

"All right." Connor straightened, resisting the need to stroke her cheek. "Let's get an X ray." He waited for Muñiz to nod and he knew that she would stay with Alix. "What happened?" he demanded of the paramedic behind him.

"Looks like a mugging, Doc, in the race-track parking lot. Possible kidnapping attempt.

We didn't find the weapon, but that's some knot on her head. Cops should be here soon." The man gave a one-fingered salute and said, "We gotta get goin'." Then he looked back at Alix. "Tiny little thing. She wouldn't stand a chance against a mugger. Hope she'll be okay."

"Alix?" He leaned down to her. "Can ye hear me?" His knuckles grazed her jaw and at last, her eyes fluttered open.

"What . . . ?" Her voice sounded rough, strange to her ears.

"Ye've had a bump on the head, sweetheart. How d'ye feel?"

Her eyebrows contracted and one hand lifted to her bandaged head. "Ouch!"

"Aye." He smiled down at her. "That'll be sore for a few days. Lift yer head now, here's sommat for the pain. We'll see later if you need something stronger." He held her while she swallowed the pills.

"What happened?" She sighed the question as he gently pushed her back down.

"They think ye were mugged. Do ye remember?"

"I remember standing beside my new car . . .

and being grabbed from behind. Not much more."

"D'ye feel up to talking to the police? They're waiting for you now."

The patrolman was blond and looked very young to her. Still, the uniform was official. She felt her breath quicken and her heart begin to pound.

"Ms. Benton?" he asked.

"Yes?" she answered unsteadily.

"I'm Officer Walker and I'll be taking your report. You were found unconscious next to your car, and the paramedics were called."

"So I understand," she said. Connor took her hand in his.

"Did you see your assailant, ma'am?" The patrolman was already writing.

"No." She paused to clear her throat. "I felt someone grab me from behind and then something hit my head. I think, as I was losing consciousness, that I was being dragged into my car."

The officer nodded. "That would be consistent with the paramedics' report. You were half in, half out of the car. It's possible that the man who found you scared away your assailant."

She looked at the white sheet beneath her and

wondered where she would be now if not for that Good Samaritan.

"I need to ask you, Ms. Benton, if you've had any dealings with drugs or gambling?"

Connor looked up fiercely and growled, "Drugs!"

The officer merely turned back to Alix. "Ma'am?"

"No," she said.

"Do you owe anybody money or have any reason to expect this kind of attack?"

"No, no, nothing like that."

"I understand you filed a report about your car being run off the road?" He continued writing.

"Y-yes, yes, that's right. A friend of mine was hurt, but she gave a description of the car. Have you found out anything?"

"No, ma'am. But it looks like you might have gotten yourself a pretty determined enemy. You might want to think about taking a vacation or going to stay with friends for a while."

"I understand," Alix said, and she was very much afraid she did.

"But you'll give her some kind of protection," Connor protested immediately. "Too many incidents have happened. There was a vandal on the track and a strange floral delivery. Then her car is run off the road and now this. The girl's obviously in danger."

The officer stared back at Connor for a moment and decided to humor him. "I'm afraid we don't even have the manpower to protect the streets, Doctor. Two vague reports that may or may not be related . . . I'm sorry, but it's not our policy to provide private security. Like I said, we just don't have the manpower."

Connor moved closer to her. "Don't worry yourself, Officer," he said in a dangerous voice. "I'll make certain the young lady comes to no harm."

A few more questions and then she was handed the report to sign. He gave her a yellow copy and a card with instructions that if she remembered anything else about the incident to please call the detective assigned to her. He then assured her that since she was a victim of a violent crime, the state of California would assist in payment of her medical bills.

Big help when he came after her again, Alix thought.

SEVEN

"Connor," Alix said urgently as soon as the patrol-man was gone.

"Lie back now, lass." He pressed her against the pillow. "You'll need to be checked every few hours. But dinna worry, I'll take care of ye. I'll take care of everything. We'll get ye home in a bit. Then I'll hire a bodyguard." He fussed with the pillow, but she sat back up again.

"Connor, listen to me. It's important." She waited until he stilled. "I think I might . . . know who's behind all this." Connor's startled eyes went from hers to where the police officer had disappeared down the hallway. Alix quickly put her hand on his wrist. "But I can't tell the police."

"What are you saying, Alixandra?"

She couldn't look at Connor directly. She didn't think her doctor with the starched shirts and perfectly creased pants was going to approve of what she had done in her desperate past.

"I'm afraid," she whispered, "that if I do, they might arrest me."

"What?" His dark brows shot up but, instinctively, he kept his own voice equally low. "What the devil are you talkin' about? Why would they arrest you?"

"Because I—I'm not," she stuttered, then shook her head. "My real name . . . isn't Alixandra Benton," she said quietly, darting searching looks at him. She licked her dry lips.

Silence. He stared down at her, his expression still, unreadable.

She couldn't know the black net that had descended over him, throwing him back to the memory of another confession. She couldn't know that his blood was freezing in his veins, stopping all thought and every emotion. In the next moment he pulled her out of bed and down the hall to his office. He closed the door behind them, pushed her into a chair, and crossed his arms over his chest. She pressed one bare foot over the other on the floor. "Say it again," he demanded in a slow, deadly stranger's voice.

"My real name isn't . . . Alixandra Benton. I

changed it when I was fifteen, in a way that could get me in trouble."

"Ye lied. By God, ye lied to me!" His expression grew more and more forbidding.

"No!" She denied it quickly. "At least, not consciously. I mean, I've been Alix Benton for so long, it never even occurred to me that there would be any reason for . . ." She faltered, not really knowing how to continue.

"No reason for the truth to come out?" He finished with a snarl.

She looked up at him. She didn't think she'd ever seen eyes so cold. "Does it really matter so much what my name is? I'm the same person I was before. That hasn't changed."

"What ye're really asking me is if it matters that ye've deceived me from the moment we met." His expression was ferocious as he glowered down at her. "Aye, it does matter! I believed you, believed *in* you, and now you tell me what was between us was less than nothing."

"Connor, I changed my name and my life ten long years ago. It's the past. Can you see that? I *am* Alixandra Benton!"

"What I see," he answered scathingly, "is a liar. There's nothing I despise more. And I'll have the truth now, all of it. You can start with whom you believe is trying to hurt you. God knows, I'd like to strangle ye myself!"

Just then a knock sounded and Nurse Muñiz poked her head in the door.

"Doctor, I'm sorry to bother you . . ."

"Aye, Muñiz," Connor said, "I'll be right along." The door closed again, and Connor turned to Alix, speaking in a slow, deliberate voice. "M'shift is over in two hours. You get yerself back into that bed and wait for me." Then he was gone.

"That's okay," Alix whispered to herself as she swallowed painfully. Hadn't she rehearsed this moment a hundred times? "I always knew it would come . . . that it couldn't last . . ."

Alix sat huddled in a tight ball on her couch, surrounded by darkness, her softball bat by her side. She'd checked the doors and windows twice but, though she felt desperately tired, she still couldn't sleep.

Suddenly, there came a great battering upon her front door. Her breath coming in short, startled gasps, she gripped the bat and rose, a little dizzy when she was upright. In another moment, she was behind the door, her heart pounding in her ears.

Biting her lip, she darted out to stare through the peephole in the center of the door.

Blackness. Nothingness.

The porch light was out. She had replaced it only last week.

Alix wet her dry lips, swallowed, and slowly, silently turned the lock. The pounding came again, followed almost immediately by an angry twisting of the brass knob. She slipped back into position, the bat high over her head.

The door opened into her dark foyer. Two feet, then a hesitation. Two feet more, and the tension was palpable. Alix felt her damp palms change to a ready position on the bat, and she drew in a deep breath. A huge, shadowed mass entered her house, and she gave a betraying cry at the same moment she brought the bat down with all the strength fear could inspire.

A huge arm blocked the blow and sent the bat flying away to bounce down the hall. Alix slid down into a ball on the floor against the wall, shivering with dread and reaction.

All motion stilled, and she lifted her chin to the darkness, awaiting the next blow.

Connor knew the difference between a bat wielded by a hundred-and-fourteen-pound woman in self-defense and one held by a determined assassin. "Bloody idiot!" he shouted.

"Connor?" she called in glad surprise.

"Damned bloody idiot," he said sotto voce this time. He reached for her and pulled her up from the floor, holding her by the shoulders. "With the door wide open! How are ye here?"

"I live here," she answered defiantly, her fear sliding away like cleansing water.

"I left ye to wait."

"You're a very old-fashioned man, Dr. MacLeod. Women in this country rarely wait for men who order them around."

"Damn ye, woman! Would ye rather be killed? I had no one to cover for me. D'ye know how I felt when they told me you were gone and I had to wait? How did you get home, then?"

She shrugged herself free of his hold and backed away. "I used the phone in your office to call a cab."

"Why?"

"I don't want to involve you. Too many things have happened. It's too dangerous."

"Ye dinna want to involve me?" His voice was outraged. "Well it's too bloody late to think o' that now!"

The air was as bitter as his voice. In the darkness he stalked her, until they were only inches apart.

"Tell me, *Ms. Beaton*, I would know the answer to a question that has occurred to me in the last few hours. Tell me what other stories have I swallowed? This Boots for one. Was he the lover before me? He wasn't a very talented teacher, was he? I'd swear ye learned more in a night with me than all yer time with him!" Rage brought the rancor to his lips, but Connor couldn't seem to help himself. He wanted to hurt her, to show her how it felt!

"Good God, Connor, I was fifteen years old!" She spun away from him. "Of course he wasn't my lover. He was my father in every way but blood. Boots took me into his house so that I wouldn't be sleeping in a stable or on the streets! He taught me everything I needed to know to be as good a jockey as I have the talent to be. He gave me confidence and self-esteem for the first time in my life." She paused, then whispered, "You're the only lover I ever had."

More lies! She was still at it, he thought, twisting her words to take him in, create sympathy. But she had manipulated him quite enough! His eyes met hers with a dark frost. "Oh, I think

I'm enough of a clinician to recognize a virgin when I give one a tumble." Disillusionment roughened his voice. He knew he was pushing her, but the anger was choking him and he was bloody well tired of playing the fool. "So, you must have had a lover sometime."

She whirled around, turning her back to him. "If you call a rapist a lover!" she snapped. "*I* don't!"

Another slam to the gut! Connor felt his heart contract in horror as he stared at the fragile column of her spine. Anger drained away. *Not that!* He reached out one hand. "Lass." He wanted to go to her, but his feet were like great stones, weighted to the floor. He felt a renewal of rage, five times more powerful than any he had felt before. His eyes closed in anguish.

For a long while neither spoke, then her voice came through the darkness. "It was the night of my birthday party. I was fifteen," she said, her back still to him.

Not Alix! he thought again, wishing it to be another lie. And he didn't want to hear, but she went on, almost conversationally.

"I lived with my aunt Maud after my parents were killed. It wasn't a . . . happy situation. One day, she told me there was to be a party, a birthday party—for me. It was the first party she . . . Maud usually didn't believe in making a fuss. But there was a band and I even made a few friends. That was great. I'd been sent away to school for years, and I didn't know anyone in Boston."

He couldn't help being surprised. She'd never mentioned a word about Boston before.

"I wasn't a very attractive fifteen," she continued, "but I had all the hopes and dreams that other girls do. My . . ." she choked on the word, "cousin had always hated me. I just never knew how much until that night."

"Yer cousin!" Connor spat the words, his outrage pouring with them. His hands fisted. "Sweet heaven!" He couldn't believe how calmly she said it.

"Bentley found me in the gazebo after the party. I've never understood his hatred. But I'd never been afraid for myself before. I should have been." Her voice caught with a sound that might have been a sob cut off, then she went on again. "After he . . . finished, he told me that if I said anything, he would tell my aunt that I had begged him to meet me, that I wanted it." Her slender shoulders gave a resigned shrug. "She always believed his word over mine," she said flatly, and suddenly he couldn't bear it anymore. He had to hold her.

He was beside her in three steps. His hands found her and turned her around. Tears streaked her face. All that time, her voice so calm and emotionless, these tears had been falling. Rage and hurt twisted inside him as he pressed her cheek to his wide shoulder.

"Och, lassie," he murmured into her hair, stroking her arms and back in clumsy motions. "I'm sorry, so verra sorry." He couldn't bear the idea of Alix being used in such a vile way, and to think it had happened when she was only a girl of fifteen. It was intolerable! However had she survived with such sweetness and open warmth intact? He gave her his handkerchief, sensing that she would rather dry her own tears just now. His eyelids burned as he asked, "What did you do? Did ye go to her?"

Alix wanted to answer him, to finish it all. But he was holding her now, sharing his strength, making her feel. Slowly, she dragged herself from his arms and moved to sit on the couch. She could only finish the story if she stopped all feeling and let the words pass through her like air from her lungs.

"I couldn't do it," she said, staring blankly

at the white tulips on the table. Connor had brought her those flowers days ago, she thought absently, and still they bloomed. "It was the only night of my life my aunt had ever approved of me. I—I just couldn't stand to see that look of approval turn to disgust. I knew she would never believe me over Bentley. And . . . I was ashamed. I thought I must have done something to make it happen. Stupid of me. But I did think it."

Silence. For a moment, Connor thought she would say no more. Then she spoke again.

"I sneaked back into the house and made it to the bathroom without being seen. I must have been in there an hour. But no matter how I scrubbed, I couldn't seem to get clean enough." She shook herself. "Anyway, when the house was quiet, I took my dog and left."

"Where did you go?"

She looked up at him. The tears had stopped. "We hitchhiked to California. I had some allowance saved. I cut my hair and, well, I've always looked so much like a boy anyway—"

He interrupted her with a rude sound.

"Boots found me mucking stalls at the track and took me in. He was the first real friend I ever had. Of course, I wasn't very trusting in the beginning." She gave a short laugh. "You should have seen his face when he found out I was a girl! I'd been living with him for about two months when he walked in on me in the shower by accident." The moon shone through a window, and she touched the petal of a tulip in its light. Her face was as still and white as a statue. "He backed out right away, but I couldn't stop screaming. He had to come in again. He wrapped me up in a towel and rocked me until I believed that I was safe. I was pretty hysterical."

The cords in Connor's neck strained, and a tic pulsed in his clenched jaw. But he had no words.

Her voice was still strangely calm. "When he heard my story, Boots got an ex-cop he knew to tell me a way I could . . . take a new identity. I committed a felony, Connor. I took a dead girl's name and got the county to send me a birth certificate for the one I'd 'lost.' With that I could get a driver's license, everything." She blushed deeply. "I know it was wrong. But if Boots hadn't made me believe I couldn't be found by Bentley or my aunt, I never would have stayed in one place for long." She looked up at him with her tear-drenched eyes. "And if I had spent the last ten years running, I doubt I'd even be alive today." She swallowed and pushed a hand through her hair.

Connor made a growling sound and swung around to the kitchen for the bottle of Scotch he kept in her cupboard. He pulled out two glasses, but splashed a healthy jolt in one and downed it before he filled them both. Then he braced himself on the counter, head bent to his chest.

The emotions churning in him were so overwhelming, he felt light-headed. He wanted to run out of the house to the woods on the mountain. He wanted to run until he couldn't feel anything. But he couldn't, wouldn't leave her.

He should have known it was something like that. That first night she'd been so unsure, so sweetly tentative and innocent. God . . . rape! He wanted to rail at the stars. Finally, after a series of calming breaths, he straightened, picked up both glasses, and went back to the living room. He flicked on the lamp by the couch.

"Here," he said, handing her a glass. Her flesh was cold where their fingers touched.

She downed the Scotch and coughed until he patted her gently between the shoulder blades. Then she wiped her mouth with the back of one trembling hand.

"You know," she said, sniffling once, "I'll get on the rankest horse and never flinch. I've gone under mounts, been thrown against the gate. I've been thrown beneath the feet of the pack and had to watch while I thought they'd trample me. I'm not a coward! But suddenly, I'm flinching at shadows again. I hear noises and spend half my time looking over my shoulder. I thought I'd never be afraid again."

"Ye're thinking it's him," Connor said quietly. "This foul cousin of yours."

She nodded.

"Why?"

"The roses that day," she said, her face pale, "the name the man said. I was born Catherine Barstow." She dug her toes into the carpet and slowly let her eyes meet his. "And today . . . I think I saw him in the stands."

Connor absorbed that, looking at her for a long moment before he said, "Right. Have you pen and paper?" When she got them, he placed them before her on the coffee table. "Now," he said, his manner completely businesslike, "I'm going to have some discreet inquiries made. I'll need you to write down all of the pertinent information. Your full name, that of your parents, your cousin, your aunt, the Boston address. What sort of business was your aunt involved in, what occupation?"

That stumped her. "I don't know." She rubbed at her temple, just below the knot on her head. It throbbed with maddening regularity.

"What do you mean?" he asked gently. He could see her head was paining her. She should be in bed.

"I don't think she worked. I mean, there was always money, we were comfortable, with servants. It was a big house. I guess her husband left her money. I remember, she had jewelry too. She wore this long strand of pearls every day." Her tongue slipped out to moisten her dry lips, lips that quivered with the toll the day had taken upon her.

Even now, knowing the falsehoods, knowing how she'd been abused, he wanted nothing so much as to bury himself in her softness. He wanted to lose himself in her fragile arms. And he wanted to kill the bastard who had hurt her, was trying to hurt her still. She was *his*, dammit! He would protect what was his.

He stood abruptly and went back into the kitchen with her glass. He brought back water and dug a package of pills out of his pocket.

"You believe me, don't you?" she asked anxiously. "I mean, you don't just think I'm some paranoid ditz. You think I'm in danger too."

"I believe you're in danger," he answered tersely. "Here." He opened the cellophane and dropped the white tablets in her palm. "If these don't manage the pain, I'll give you something else that will."

"Thanks." She smiled faintly as she looked up at him.

He straightened. "I want you to pack a few things and come down to my house tonight. It has a good alarm system. We can go through the backyard. Leave the lights on here." He looked her over carefully. "Would you rather I pack for you?"

"You don't want me there," she said. "It's not fair to involve you. Really, Connor, I'll be all right. Tomorrow I'll hire a great big, mean ole bodyguard. I didn't do it tonight because it was so late. I'll be fine."

"If I pack, ye'll get naught but a toothbrush and change of clothes," he threatened, as if she'd never said a word.

She studied his stern face, tracing each strong feature with loving eyes. He was a good man, a kind man, strong and true. Who wouldn't fall in love with such a man?

"Okay." She gave in with a tired sigh. "Just for tonight." She rubbed her temple again. "I'll get my things."

He took her through the backyards of their neighbors, lifting her over a low hedge before she even tried it herself. When he released her, her hands lingered on his shoulders, clinging despite her best intentions.

"Come." He took her hand again and they passed through Mrs. Temple's garden. He steered her around the rosebushes and then they were in his yard.

He punched a series of buttons in the panel on the wall that surrounded his patio. The red light on the panel went out. A short, shrill beep sounded, and he pulled her to the back door.

Inside, she was surprised to see that he had chosen varying shades of beige, wheat, and taupe for his decor. It was airy and calm, but curiously unlike him. She had pictured dark woods, midnight-blue and burgundy. She turned to him, grinning.

"You did the decorating?"

"No," he answered sheepishly. "I'm not much for that sort o' thing. I asked the wife of a colleague to pick out some things for me." He blinked, uncertain. "What do you think?"

"It's nice," she said diplomatically.

"Looks like a doctor's office," he grumbled.

She laughed, and the sound settled in the base of his spine. "A very expensive doctor's office."

Their eyes met and the moment grew uncomfortable. Connor reached for her suitcase, which he had placed beside him.

"You should be in bed," he said as he set out for the hall. "I'll put you in the guest room."

At his words, her face flamed brilliant rose. *He didn't want her anymore!* She felt humiliated. She had envisioned sleeping safely surrounded by his hard arms and furnace heat. She knew he was upset at what he felt was her deliberate deception. But when he'd asked her to come to his house, she had thought, had hoped, he might have forgiven her. Head down, she followed him to his guest room.

Connor placed her suitcase on a chair and turned in time to see her swaying before the bed. With a low oath, he swung her into his arms, then laid her on the bed.

"I'm all right, Con," she whispered.

He ignored her, turning away to pull a nightgown from her suitcase. When he returned, she held the top button of her cotton shirt closed.

"I—I can do it," she stammered, refusing him.

He stared down at her, astonished. "I've seen

ye before, lass," he said, his voice harsher than he meant it to be.

But you wanted me then, her heart cried silently. She didn't have the strength for further protests. The day had simply been too traumatic. Connor made quick work of getting her out of her clothes, and she blushed right down to the tips of her breasts when she wore only her lace panties. He dropped the thin cotton gown over her head and guided her arms through in a very professional manner. But if she had only had the courage to look at him, she might have seen the effect she had on his body.

He slipped her beneath the covers, repositioned her pillows, and turned out the bedside light. "I'll leave the door open a bit and the hall light on," he said as he left.

The next day, Connor took time off from the clinic. He had asked Carlotta to find him a replacement the night before, and there wasn't a doubt in his mind as to her efficiency. After a call to a friend with a somewhat obscure occupation, he found a detective agency that could supply him both detective and bodyguard. Then he called his lawyer.

Alix slept until ten o'clock, waking only because Connor brought her coffee. He sat next to her on the bed.

"Good morning," he said gently.

Her lashes fluttered, and he was the first thing she saw. He looked strong and imperturbable. The steaming cup he held seemed small in his big hands.

"Oh." She pushed the hair out of her eyes and slid the strap of her nightgown back up over her shoulder. He watched every move, but she couldn't read his expression. "Thank you," she said primly, sitting up, the covers clasped tight. She took the coffee from him without touching his fingers.

"Your bodyguard is due to arrive in a bit," he said, smiling, "and I thought you might wish to be dressed for the occasion."

"Thanks." She smiled back, and he left her to it.

When she was ready, she found him in the living room.

"Is there more coffee?" she asked shyly.

"Yes." He turned to her from the wide patio doors that looked into the woods. "Would you like me to get it for you?"

"No, that's okay. I can find it."

The awkwardness between them gave her a sad, funny feeling as she walked toward the kitchen. She hadn't realized he'd followed her until she began to fill her cup and found his beside it on the counter. She almost dropped the pot.

"Caution, lass." He waited until she had filled both cups, then said, "Let's sit for a moment, there are things I would like to discuss with you." They sat at the kitchen table. "In addition to a bodyguard, a private detective will look into your family's background and the whereabouts of your cousin."

Alix blinked. "Fast work."

"We have an appointment this afternoon with my lawyer." He saw the panic in her eyes. "No fear, a lawyer will advise us with absolute confidentiality."

After a moment she nodded. "All right."

The doorbell rang. The bodyguard had arrived.

EIGHT

His name was Turk Madden. He was six feet four inches tall, with massive shoulders and cool silver eyes. He had long, shaggy hair the color of molten honey, wore a brown bomber jacket, and carried a briefcase. A small white scar ran through his left eyebrow. He looked dangerous, as if he had learned his lessons early in terrible circumstances. But Alix trusted him almost immediately.

Standing in the same room with the two men made her feel like a midget, but there was an obvious difference between them. Turk's eyes revealed none of the gentleness that always lingered in the depths of Connor's.

Turk seemed a careful man, deliberate in both motion and words. He called her "Miss Benton" when introduced.

"Call me Alix." She held out a hand.

"Turk," he answered solemnly, enveloping her hand in his huge palm. Then he turned to Connor. "The first thing I'd like to do is make sure the perimeter is secure." He waited for Connor to nod his agreement. He nodded in return and stepped past them to make his survey. A few minutes later, he joined them in the kitchen.

"Security system is a bit antiquated, but should be adequate to give warning of a break-in. The windows have a touch-sensitive option, so we'll be using the central air and heat full-time from now on." He looked from Alix to Connor. "Do either of you know how to use a gun?"

"No!" Alix answered quickly, appalled at the idea. She was surprised when Connor made a sound of assent and said, "But I dinna keep one."

Turk unbuckled his belt and pulled it free. A holstered gun was attached so that it rested behind his waist. He handed the apparatus to Connor and said, "Baretta. It's legal on my permit as long as it stays in the house. I'd prefer the lady have the larger bedroom. I'll take the couch. Then we'll be on either side of her. With the frequency of these incidents, my guess is they'll try for her again, whether we provide an easy target or a difficult one. After so many attempts, we have to assume they're going to be desperate."

Connor swallowed that thoughtfully. "Alix and I have an appointment in Pasadena this afternoon."

"Negative," Turk answered. "If it's essential, I can call in additional men. But you don't want Alix to be a road target again if you can help it."

"Aye," Connor said. "I'll go alone then." He gave Alix a reassuring glance. "I'll only be gone an hour and a half, two at the most."

Alix looked back at Connor, at his kind face and sure strength. She wondered how much danger he might be in because of her.

"Turk?" Alix called as she came into the living room. She had on a T-shirt and shorts with tennis shoes. Her hands were clasped nervously before her. Turk was sprawled on the couch, reading a magazine.

"Yes, ma'am?" He sat up with the speed of a panther. Now that he had taken off his jacket, his holstered gun was clearly nestled against one shoulder.

She blinked quickly, sure she would lose her nerve if she didn't get it right out. "I—I don't know how to use a gun. I don't even think I want to know how."

"I understand." Turk leaned back and watched her. She was from a different world than his, where guns were something seen on television.

"But," she went on, her hands moving in nervous, fluttering motions, "I wonder if you could show me anything like . . . well, maybe a couple of self-defense moves. I—I just felt so helpless when that guy caught me from behind in the parking lot. I didn't like it. I don't want to dream about it."

Scarcely a beat passed before Turk asked, "You're right-handed?" as if he already knew the answer. He unfolded his length from the couch and took two steps to the center of the wide room.

"Yes," Alix answered, trying to hide her trepidation.

"Fine, then your right leg is your strong leg. This is important. In any confrontation, you want to plant your right leg back and keep your weak leg forward. Someone approaches you from the front, keep your hand waist-high. That way you

have a hand free if you see they have a weapon.
Try that, now."

For the first time, he really took her measure.
She was scared, true, but he saw strength of character in her delicate features and the determined
set of her chin. He decided she would handle
herself all right.

He gave her a level look and tried to impart
some of his own confidence to her. "Okay, Alix.
I'm approaching from the front. With your height
and weight, the best bet for you is a kick to the
groin. Like this." He demonstrated the kick with
a force she couldn't imagine being able to imitate.
"Try it." She did. It was a weak imitation. "You'd
better try a little higher or you'll give him nothing
but a shin splint."

"Wouldn't I kick him with my knee?" she
asked, hoping that would make her stronger. She
made a wry face. "That's what they always seem
to do in the movies."

It was the first grin she'd seen on Turk's
craggy face. She tried not to stare, but it seemed
strangely out of place. It changed him, made him
more human.

"You'll get a good deal more force with your
foot, unless you're in a clinch and don't have
the room. But the truth is, most attacks upon
women do come from behind. Like this." He

moved around her and caught her in a loose choke hold.

"Okay, you got me," she said, trying not to imagine Bentley in that position. What shocked her was that she felt no revulsion at Turk's touch, or to the musky scent of him that surrounded her. The sense of belonging she felt in Connor's arms was missing, but she felt nothing that made her skin crawl. She set her mouth purposefully. "What do I do?"

"When an assailant's got you in a choke, he's leaning a bit forward, usually off balance. This is where your lack of height will work for you. So, you plant your strong leg back to help you keep your own balance secure. Then you either shove yourself back against him, or forward. I'd say forward is better for you. That will give you room to twist sideways, then kick backward with your right leg. If you feel you have a better chance pushing back against your attacker, you have to move fast. Shove back, then forward, and perform the same kick." He demonstrated both kicks fast, then in a kind of slow motion. "It'll take some practice, but it's worth the effort." He gave her another appraising glance. "We'll try it again tomorrow, and I'll show you a couple more moves."

"Thank you." She smiled at him, and Turk spent a moment envying the doctor. She had guts, this pretty little girl, he'd give her that.

Connor was pleased with what he'd learned from his lawyer. He could hardly wait to tell Alix. He let himself into the house after giving the knock-ring-knock signal he and Turk had agreed upon.

Even though Connor had a key, Turk met him at the door. His shirtsleeves were rolled up. "Quiet afternoon."

"Good," Connor answered. "Where's Alix?"

"In the kitchen." Turk eyed him as he said carefully, "We're making dinner."

That caught Connor's attention. "You are." He straightened and gave Turk a look men somehow always understood. It was both challenge and "keep out."

One corner of Turk's hard mouth turned up. "I'm a gourmet Chinese chef."

Connor's eyes lit with amusement. The last thing the man looked like was any type of chef. "Mandarin or Szechuan?"

"Szechuan."

"Splendid. I'm quite hungry."

All through dinner, and it was gourmet, Connor watched the ease with which Alix and Turk dealt with each other. He'd only been gone a couple of hours, yet a strange, affectionate rapport had been built between them. He didn't much care for it.

Over the last of the green tea, Connor finally said, "Alix, if you don't mind, I'd like to have a few words with you in private."

Before Turk could rise from his chair, Alix asked, "About what your lawyer said? Don't worry about Turk. I explained my strange past to him while you were gone."

A thrust of envy or anger—he wasn't sure which—hit him square-on. It had taken a threat to her life for Alix to tell him her secrets, yet she'd told them to Turk after knowing him a single day. He cleared his throat and tried not to let his emotions show.

"Fine, then. My lawyer doesn't believe you have anything to worry about. When you used a false birth certificate you did commit a felony. But the statute of limitations on that kind of fraud is five years. We can go to the police now." He watched her reward him with a beaming smile of relief.

"Thank you. I've been so nervous about

it." She leaned forward and pressed his hand. Connor's whole self warmed as he turned his hand over and held hers. But he pulled back when he felt Turk's speculative gaze upon them.

Later that night, when Alix had gone to bed, Connor and Turk played cards in the living room. Connor sat close to the hallway and had one ear tuned to the open door of his bedroom, where Alix slept. He listened to the soft rustlings as she tossed and turned for nearly an hour. Finally, he looked at Turk and put down his cards.

"I believe I'll say good night," he said casually.

"I'll be here." Turk nodded in understanding and reached for the television remote control. He watched Connor walk down the hall and smiled faintly to himself.

"Ye're nervous," Connor said matter-of-factly from the bedroom doorway. He could see Alix's outline against the headboard as she sat up. When she reached to turn on the light, he saw the wild look in her eyes that matched the untamed mass of sun-streaked hair that drifted over her shoulders, over her breasts. She wore a sleeveless cotton nightgown with a drawstring laced through the bodice. He closed the door behind him.

"I'm sorry." She pushed her hair back in a thoughtlessly sensual gesture and sighed. "I can't seem to stop thinking about it, about Bentley, wondering why."

He strode over to the bed and looked down at her. She looked up at him curiously, unsure of him and the strange expression on his face. Too, she'd never seen him in such informal clothing—cotton trousers and a white T-shirt—except when he was completely unclothed. That thought distracted her until, with a flick of his wrist, he peeled away her sheet and coverlet, tossing them high. Her gaze followed the motion as they floated to the floor at the bottom of the bed.

"Connor?" Her startled eyes met his. "What . . . ?"

"I'm going to help ye sleep," he said enigmatically.

Her lips twitched with amusement as she straightened the cotton gown over her thighs. "You don't look like a sleeping pill to me."

"No?" he asked, a glint in his dark eyes as he sat down beside her. She was still looking at him with a puzzled expression when he reached for the thin satin ribbon of her gown and untied the bow. One hand slipped into the opened vee and cupped a breast, grazing a nipple that hardened instantly to his touch. A tremor ran through her, and he bent to kiss her lips as she arched into his hand.

It was expert, as kisses go, with the sensuous flavor that all of Connor's kisses contained. It went on and on as he tasted her, lips nibbling, tongue finding the corners of her mouth, and finally, finally slipping inside her wet warmth to explore further. But there was something wrong with the kiss. As arousing and wonderful as it might be, something was missing that had always been there before, some bit of Connor himself. Alix suddenly realized that this kiss was sex, not love, or even the deep, wondering affection that had always been between them. She couldn't help but be stirred by him. Yet something in her rebelled at his being so cool and casual about an act that had always carried such an emotional impact for them both.

"No." She twisted, trying to push him away, but without success. "Not like this."

"Shhh," he hushed her, lightly massaging her burning nipples. Both hands were inside her gown now as he bit the side of her neck.

A small moan left her throat, and she felt her temperature rise, felt herself weakening. "No," she said again, though it sounded more like a sigh. "You don't want me . . ." But then one of his hands was sliding up her bare thigh and she couldn't think of what she'd been going to say.

"Always," he whispered against her mouth. He took her bottom lip between his teeth, sucking it gently. "I always want you." His thumb found the moist warmth between her thighs and explored there in tantalizing, erotic motions. He rubbed tight, ever-smaller circles, and his other hand squeezed her breast in the same rhythm as his mouth devoured hers.

"But . . . Turk?" she murmured against him.

"He knows where we are."

Her body had taken over her reason. "I . . . oh!" She could only whimper softly as he bent to suckle at one swollen, sensitive breast, then the other. Her nerves were drawn taut and lightning rods of reaction connected her nipples to her womb with each motion of his mouth upon her. Drugged with sensation, she heard his low groan as he lavished each breast with equal attention; licking, biting, drawing with deep, nearly painful, suction until the sighing sounds she made satisfied him. Then his long fingers slid deep inside her, and she flexed around them, clenching her inner muscles. When he tried to withdraw his hand, she followed the motion down to keep him inside her until she was flat on the bed, her nightgown hiked up around her waist.

Connor looked down at her and smiled. Her face was flushed, eyes closed, full lips parted in anticipation. Sweat dampened her temples and a strand of hair was caught there. His fingers moved slowly in and out of her burning heat, as his other hand dragged the nightgown up and over her head. He used that same hand to free himself of his trousers, never stopping the play between her sweetly spread thighs.

His mouth sought her breast again, and she loosed a muffled cry that made him draw harder until she shook with a startling, shuddering release. Slowly, in gentle motions, he brought her down. Then he kissed her again, absorbing her little murmurings into his own mouth.

He kissed his way across her silky cheek to nip at her earlobe, then his tongue dipped in and traced the delicate whorls. "Och, the sweetness of ye, lassie." His voice was amazed.

That easily, she was aroused again, yearning for more.

Connor let his hot kisses drift down her slender throat, over her breastbone, down to the rounded curves of her breasts and ripe, swollen nipples.

His fingers began to move again between her legs, slowly, so slowly, until her hips shifted restlessly. His burning lips had trailed down to her little belly, and he tongued her navel and kissed each hipbone, before he moved on to the damp nest of curls.

She gasped when he lifted her legs over his shoulders, because she knew that in the next second his mouth would be upon her. And so it was, a fiery brand of possession and certain knowledge of her response. His tongue caressed her, then his lips, and she gave a tiny sob of defeat as his callused fingers kneaded the silky cheeks of her bottom.

Her hands grabbed at the sheet beneath her in torment as it went on and on until there was no time, until her body was shaking, completely out of control.

She was rising, flying higher into ecstasy than ever before when suddenly, he stopped. Her eyes flew open and she tried to control her gasping breaths.

"Do ye want me?" he rasped out in a low voice.

"Yes," she whispered, and was rewarded with a kiss. After all that he had done to her, it was a teasing agony. "I want you," she said, and was rewarded with another.

He lowered her to the bed and reached for the bedside drawer. She watched him through half-closed lids, muttering, "Hurry!"

He looked back and there was both amusement and hunger in his eyes. Her own fell shut as she heard the ripping sound of foil. Then she felt his weight upon the bed again. Connor looked at her flushed cheeks, her moist pink lips, then downward. His heart was pounding, his manhood aching, and still he waited.

When her eyes opened again, he stared into their blue-green depths and absorbed her vulnerability, her need. Tenderness flooded him. As he leaned down to kiss her, her fists opened long enough to find his strong shoulders and grasp them. His mouth moved over hers as he reached between her legs with one hand. He cupped her tightly, then rolled the swollen nub between two fingers as she groaned again.

"I can't stand it, Connor!" Her legs drew together, needing to capture him against her, to keep that agonizing, delicious pressure. "Please!" she begged raggedly.

She felt him parting her legs, lifting them over his shoulders once more. Then he was inside her, hot and throbbing, filling her completely. She moaned her relief and arched her back as he began to move. "Yes!" she sighed at the burning friction of each plunge. With only the fourth thrust she was convulsing around him. He didn't stop, didn't slow, but drove into her again and again, until she was in a frenzy once more. When he felt her pushing up against him, he took her legs from his shoulders and wrapped them around his waist.

Now he slowed to a different rhythm, one that stroked, circled, and tantalized as he caressed the satin skin of her waist, her breasts. He murmured praise words, her name, what he wanted from her.

Alix stroked his sweat-slicked back, his chest, and the taut bands of his stomach. Her hands slid to his hips and his sexy, contoured backside. It was when her hands slid between them, cradling the heavy, rounded sac, letting her nails scrape lightly, that his control shattered.

He became wild, driving into her with relentless, thrilling force. Twisting his body, moving hers to his pleasure, he slammed into her, pounding, thrusting, his gentleness a thing of the past. Alix came and came again until she was sobbing aloud at the joy of it, until at last he lunged, pressing deep against her womb. He bit her neck, drawing the tender skin between his teeth, sucking hard. When he released it, he had left his mark upon her and the sight of it sent him over the edge. With a low, anguished cry he convulsed above her and collapsed.

"The devil!" The words burst from Connor as soon as he came to his senses. He rolled away and leaned over Alix, still panting, bracing himself on one elbow. Her eyelashes were dark lace against her cheeks, and he felt an overwhelming surge of emotion, part tenderness, part guilt. He hadn't intended to lose himself in her like that. He hadn't wanted to feel the crazed possessiveness that had taken him over. He had thought to give them both an uncomplicated, physical release, something that obviously wasn't possible between them. Sweet heaven! Would she equate him with that damned rapist now?

"Alix! Alixandra!"

Her eyes opened at the urgency of his tone.

"Are ye . . . did I hurt ye?"

"No." She smiled at the exquisite sensations still tingling her nerves. "You never hurt me."

Then she realized he was truly concerned. She rolled to face him, curving one hand over his rough cheek. But his eyes lit upon the red mark on her neck, then the other marks his fingers had left upon her arms. He cursed under his breath and was gone from her bed in the next instant.

Shocked, eyes wide with disbelief and confusion, Alix watched him jerk his pants up over his hips, the T-shirt over his head. Then, without even looking at her, he left, the door closing with a solid, metallic click.

Alix stared after him, lips trembling. Then she turned and buried her face in his pillow.

Connor stalked down the hall to the other bedroom and quietly closed the door behind him, unwilling to face Turk in the living room. He walked over to the window and pushed the curtain aside, staring into the darkness.

He was disgusted with himself. He had always thought he was a man of discipline. He'd prided himself on his sense of control. He wasn't a violent man. His choices weren't made by his emotions or his body's needs. Nevertheless, his needs had controlled him that night.

He didn't remember ever feeling the kind of anger he had felt when Alixandra had first confessed her lies. But he would never have taken her in anger. No, it had taken jealousy, lust, and possessiveness combined to drive him to her. And he'd hurt her. Dear God, he was twice her size and he'd driven into her like a crazed animal! A quick shudder of memory ran through him, a physical residue of the pleasure she had given him. The only thing that saved his sanity was the echoing memory of her cries of satisfaction.

Connor's mind was a black muddle. With a savage shake of his head, he stormed from the room, heading for the kitchen and his whisky.

Turk had been lying on the couch, watching television, when Connor had passed through to the kitchen. Looking at the bottle on the counter, he decided that any company was better than the condemning solitude of his own thoughts. Taking the bottle with him, he walked back into the living room.

"A dram?" he asked curtly.

Turk made a careful study of Connor's face. His lips looked full and blurred, a flush still colored his cheekbones. He had obviously come straight from Alix's bed, and he didn't look any too happy about it.

"On duty," Turk answered. "But sit." He watched the big Scot settle on a wide chair and pour himself a shot. "She's a nice little girl," he said, trying to open up the conversation.

Connor stopped the glass at his lips and looked menacing. "Aye, that she is. And she's taken." As soon as he said the words, Connor felt like an idiot caveman. But he wouldn't take them back.

"That right?" Turk couldn't resist asking. He saw the way Alix and Connor looked at each other, felt the tension every time they were in a room together. He had relinquished any interest in Alix the first time he saw their eyes so deliberately avoid each other. But that didn't mean he liked being warned off.

Connor slammed back the whisky. "I'll tell ye once, Mr. Madden." He glared at the other man. "That lass is *my* lass. Ye can accept that as fact or we can continue this discussion another way."

Turk gave a one-sided smile. Damned if he didn't like the man. "Do you think you could best me, Doctor?" He leaned forward on his elbows.

Connor sat back and relaxed. "Whether I did or no, Mr. Madden, the lass would still be mine."

Now Turk's smile was full-blown. "Call me

Turk." And with those words, both men knew the game was over.

"My friends call me Connor," Connor said as he gave an answering grin.

A few minutes of comfortable silence passed before Connor spoke again. "Can we protect her?"

"How long did you have in mind?" Turk asked in a slow drawl.

"What the devil else can I do?" Connor slammed the glass against the table so hard, it bounced back into the air before he caught it.

Turk could see that the lack of choices was torturing the man. "I called the office a few minutes ago. According to his personal secretary, Barstow is vacationing on Fiji. Do you believe Alix saw him at Santa Anita?"

Connor fingered the empty glass, looking into its shallow distortions. Then he banged it on the table again. "Aye, I do."

"When he learns about the inquiries from the police, he'll realize his cover's been blown. He might fold up his tent, or he might set himself up with a whale of an alibi and hire somebody else to do the job. Or, he could do something really stupid." The look he gave Connor was the look of a predator. "Me, I'd like him to do something stupid. I've had people check the major hotels, his credit cards, but so far, no luck."

Connor shoved his fingers through his hair and made a low, growling noise. "Give me a few days. If he doesn't make his move, we'll talk about this again."

The next morning, Alix joined the two men in the kitchen for breakfast. Turk glanced at Connor, one eyebrow lifted at the reddened mark on her neck and whisker burns on her chin. But Connor was busy looking at the dark circles and puffiness around her eyes. When he finally realized where Turk's gaze had landed, he flushed and stuffed half a piece of toast in his mouth.

She was lovely, Connor thought, with her hair flowing over her shoulders in those tangled, feminine curls and her big turquoise eyes that saw right to the heart of a man. He looked at the mark he had made upon her neck in passion, then his eyes met hers and heat flared again.

Alix didn't understand Connor, but she saw the desire for her in his eyes. He had come to her the night before as if he couldn't stay away, but he hadn't stayed and he had yet to say a word about his feelings for her. *If* he had feelings for her. As for herself, she was deeply in love, without a hope of heaven. Still, she was his while he wanted her.

"Good morning," she said carefully.

"Good morning." Turk was the one to answer her. "I'm glad you're up. We have a few things to discuss."

After updating Alix, Turk made two calls and an hour later the police detective assigned to Alix's case showed up at the house. Connor stood tall and silent behind her chair as she made her statement. She didn't mention her fraudulent ID to the detective, but she did tell him her real name. The detective gave her a speculative glance, but he only said they would have the Boston authorities question her cousin.

Meanwhile, Turk's people had had a chance to do a bit more digging.

"Alix, Connor." He called for them to join him in the living room twenty minutes later. "Bingo—we've got a motive. Maud Barstow died seven months ago, leaving Bentley set to inherit the thirty-five million dollars that had been left in trust to Catherine Barstow by her father." Turk watched Alix's eyes widen in surprise, then he continued. "The trust will be broken on her twenty-fifth birthday. But Bentley can inherit only if he can get Catherine declared legally dead. If Catherine Barstow is found alive, he'll have to 'make do' with the seven million Mummy left him."

"Bastard!" Connor hissed.

Turk gave him a look of complete understanding and said to Alix, "I've asked for a picture of him from the *Globe* files. He's got too much money not to be socially prominent." He paused, then said, "Your cousin's started proceedings to declare you legally dead."

Connor thinned his lips. "I'll have my lawyer let them know the lady is alive and well."

"She'll probably have to go to Boston," Turk answered, "to the court itself and produce early medical records, dental, blood tests." He looked at Alix. "You got all that stuff?"

Alix looked back, startled. "No, I left with nothing. I don't . . ."

Connor frowned. "See what you can remember, Alixandra. Write it down; doctors' names, locations. We'll work it out from there. And your blood tests will help."

Just then there came a quick knock at the door. Turk went immediately to battle stance. He signaled for Connor and Alix to move toward the pantry, away from the windows, as he pulled his gun and went to the door. One eye to the peephole and he clicked the lock upward.

Jake Knowles, one of his best men, stood there with a tiny, cursing woman squirming in his hands. She had two black eyes and tape across her nose. "Let me go, you big gorilla!" she hollered as she tried to stomp Jake's toes.

Turk looked amused and motioned them inside. Jake swung the woman up into the air and across the threshold.

Alix rushed around the corner to the foyer. She had recognized Dani's voice. Connor was just behind her, trying to hold her back.

"Dani!" Alix exclaimed. "What are you doing here?"

"I found her snooping around Ms. Benton's house, Turk . . ." Jake started.

"Yeah," Dani spat back at Turk. "And before I could open my mouth, this behemoth grabs me and carts me down here like a sack of oats!" She turned her attention to Alix. "You okay, kid? They haven't hurt you, have they?"

Alix smiled at Dani's concern. "This is Turk Madden, Dani, my bodyguard."

"Hmmph," Dani answered, rubbing her wrists and taking the measure of the man. "He looks like a crook," she finally said.

Alix grinned at Turk. "I sort of think that's the idea."

Turk's eyes flashed his own amusement, but his mouth remained an uncompromising slash. "What were you doing at the house, ma'am?" he asked politely.

Dani looked him over again and turned back to Alix. "You didn't answer my calls, and with all the weird stuff that's been happening, I had to come by and find out if you were okay."

Turk wasn't a man who often had the experience of being ignored. He found it . . . interesting, and took a second look at the child with the broken nose. She'd probably been punched by someone who didn't warm up to her manners.

Alix smiled warmly. It was nice to have somebody who cared if she didn't surface. "Thanks, brat." She looked from Connor to Turk. "Connor thought it'd be safer here while we figure this thing out. How 'bout a cup of coffee?"

"Sure," Dani answered, hooking one arm in Alix's as they walked toward the kitchen. She glanced at her friend's neck and asked blithely, "So who gave you the hickey, the doc or the crook?"

NINE

Dani insisted on spending the night, for "moral support." Still, considering the whisker burns, she was surprised to find herself sharing Connor's big bed with Alix.

The following day, copies of Bentley's picture arrived with one of Turk's people. They all gathered around the coffee table while Turk laid out the society articles. Alix stared down at her cousin's too good-looking face. Here was the man who wanted money so badly, he was ready to kill his own cousin for it. Funny, she thought, he wasn't so changed. He looked like a mild-mannered stockbroker, handsome in a tux. And he was smiling.

Dani's comment was concise. "Slime-ball."

Alix stood up and left the room. Connor met

Turk's eyes and Dani's, bruised and so filled with concern. Then he got up to follow his woman.

Alix paced the bedroom, then finally faced the window. She had decided she'd had enough. She was tired of feeling like a pincushion while someone else waited with the pins.

Connor came up behind her. She knew it was him, as she knew the warm breadth of his body when he moved close, so close.

"I won't let that bastard hurt you, lass," he said in his low, confident doctor's voice.

She raised her hand to the curtain, then let it drift down. "I'm not your responsibility, Connor."

"Think again, then!" he snapped, this time all male arrogance. Before she could draw another breath, he had pulled her against his wide, warm chest. He held her there, just stroking the jumbled silk of her hair for a long time.

Turk, of course, had sensed it coming, even before Alix spoke to him. Cabin fever was a hazard in his trade. And this was one courageous lady. Alix made her announcement at dinner that night.

"What the devil are you talking about?" Connor demanded.

Alix was unperturbed by his angry tone. "Just what I said. I'm riding tomorrow."

"Don't be ridiculous! Your life is more important than a race!" Connor's expression was completely forbidding

"Look, Connor. I know you don't like what I do, but I have people depending on me." She felt the tension in her own body, but she knew what she had to do. "The Derby is tomorrow and I'm riding Pride of Place!"

"So sudden? This race is the one ye have to ride? Dinna give me more stories, Alixandra!"

"Okay!" She tossed her head, long hair flying over her shoulder. "The truth! You want your precious truth? If I say the words, will it make you see it? How long can I hide out here with you and Turk?" She watched Connor exchange a glance with the other man, who gave an almost imperceptible shake of his head that only angered her. "The *truth* is that I'm not safe. Not here with you, not anywhere! And you're not safe with me! Bentley has disappeared. My birthday is two months away. I can either stay here and let you continue to coddle me into believing I'm safe for the number of days that I can swallow it, or I can bring in more of Turk's people and set a trap for him."

Connor stared at her for a long moment, then he looked to Turk, who returned his steady gaze. He felt his gut tighten with apprehension. But finally, heart heavy, he said, "Verra well."

It rained the next morning. Not a spring shower, but a steady downpour.

"Ye cannot be riding in this torrent?" Connor was astonished as she met him in the living room at five A.M., ready to leave for the early workout.

Connor's eyelids were heavy, she noticed, as if he hadn't slept. She caught a glimpse of Turk and Dani in the kitchen, pouring coffee into an army-size thermos.

"Of course I am." She gave him an indulgent look. "If we waited for sunshine, we wouldn't race for a third of the season. Don't worry, the horses are trained in all kinds of weather, they know what to do." She lifted her windbreaker, ready to put her arm through the sleeve, when it was snatched from her hands as she was whirled around.

"Don't worry!" He grabbed her arms and said in a low, frustrated voice, "I worry!" Her startled eyes met his for a second before he slammed his mouth down upon hers. He kissed her deeply, hungrily. His tongue thrust into her mouth and possessed every bit of her heat.

He shook with the instant force of his arousal, and her arms rose to cling to his broad shoulders so tightly, she was lifted off her feet. Again and again, he kissed her. His mouth played with hers, nipping, sliding back and forth. Then he was pressing the warm juncture of her thighs against his hard, aching arousal.

She wanted him! She wanted his heat, his power, deep inside her. She needed him to be a part of her. Her legs rose and clasped his hips in an effort to get closer. She was filled with an urgency she'd never known, so deep it was a pain inside her.

Whimpering against the lush warmth of his mouth, she never gave a thought to the fact that Turk and Dani were only fifteen feet away. Connor was moving toward his bedroom with a speed she hardly noticed, for she was kissing him over and over, everywhere; mouth, eyes, nose, chin. She was like something wild.

"You're so beautiful, so strong," she breathed between kisses. "All of you, shoulders, your arms—" She tore at his tieless shirt. "Your thighs and here . . ." Her hand shaped his rigid length, and a shock of heat ran through her. "So hard and wonderful. But inside, Connor," she sighed against his lips. "Inside, you are even more beautiful." She whispered again, "Beautiful."

Blood rushed through him at a frantic rate. He had the door closed and locked behind them without ever knowing how it happened. He couldn't believe the things she was saying to him! He felt powerful and uncivilized, with a strange kind of magic.

No sooner had he put her on the bed than she had his pants unzipped. Her clever hands were surrounding him, coaxing him to even greater heat. A drop of liquid pearled the tip of his shaft, and his breath came in great gasps.

He was staggered by the passion in her, the passion she drew from him. He had her lace-trimmed T-shirt off and her jeans open in frantic moments. He tore her bra away and she was senseless by the time he pushed her legs back down and shoved her jeans to her ankles. He fell over her as he pulled her boots off, panting hard.

Connor paused just long enough to look down at her, at her sweetly formed limbs, the delicacy of her face, her breasts, her wrists and ankles. He smiled at the supple, athletic strength of her.

Tears seeped from the corners of her eyes as she met his gaze. Her arms lifted. He was more than she had ever dreamed of wanting, more than she could ever have.

He quivered with the force of his restraint as he guided his hot, hard length to her warmth and rested there.

"Now!" she cried softly, her hands dragging at his hips. "Hard, Connor!" She arched high, and he was inside her, filling her until he touched the edge of her womb. His first plunge made her sob, but he thrust again and again. She shook with the intensity of her emotions and had to bite her lip to keep from blurting out words of love.

He lunged forward and clasped her tightly, kissing her again, biting at her swollen mouth, sucking her lower lip. He groaned deeply, then suddenly pulled away, leaving her. Ignoring her instant protest, he flipped her onto her stomach in one smooth motion. With one palm upon her taut belly, he drew her upward until she was on her hands and knees. Bewildered, Alix looked back over one shoulder, but in that instant he was inside her again, biting her neck, moving in an agonizing dance while his fingers slid around her hip and down her stomach. Finding her woman's flesh through the soft blond curls, he began to tease her with every thrust.

Instinct guided her as she arched her back and pushed against his thrusts. Rising to her knees, she put her hands on his hips behind her. She felt his muscles shift under her fingers as he surged forward, over and over. Then he grabbed her hips and pumped frantically until he felt her enclose him in the shuddering heat of her climax. Groaning, he clasped her tight, one hand upon her breast as he came and came and came inside her.

Alix stroked his hair some minutes later as her heartbeat began to slow. The thick waves curled around her fingers, and she bent closer to breathe in his rich, musky scent. Sighing, she closed her eyes and murmured, "That's what it's like."

"Mmm?" The sound was all the answer he could manage. He was drained, of emotion and energy, yet he felt curiously joyous, curiously light.

"What we just shared, the way it felt. That's what it's like to race and win. I mean, to have a magnificent, talented thoroughbred be a part of you, to be one with such passion and energy . . . and then to *win* . . . against all others and all the odds! It's like flying, like no other kind of freedom!" She rolled onto his chest and smiled, putting a hand to his face. She sighed again, happy, relieved. "Really, that's what it's like. And I'm so glad . . . you know now."

Suddenly full of emotion he didn't understand, he dragged her to him, kissing the top of her head as he held her close.

The rain was only a drizzle by the time they got to Santa Anita, but even a drizzle makes for a muddy track.

Before they'd left, Turk had made sure they each had their instructions for the day. He handed Alix a small canister and said, "I know you can't wear a bullet proof vest because of the weight. But you should be able to tuck this into your waistband. It's a substance called *dye-witness*. It'll shoot a green foam that expands instantly. You can use it up to about ten feet away, but only once, so aim for the eyes. It'll blind an assailant for a few precious moments." Turk grinned. "And the guy won't be able to wash the green dye off his skin for seven days."

Her eyes lit with pleasure at the idea.

Sammy had gotten her six mounts to race that day, though the big stakes were, of course, for the eighth race. The Derby. Alix worked each of the horses she was to ride that day.

Sammy knew the truth now, and she didn't like to see the worry on his worn face because of it.

"I've got lots of big mean guys to protect me, you know," she said quietly, when she took him aside.

The fat cigar broke in his hand, and Sammy looked disgusted at his display of nerves. "Just see that they do their job, kid. My money's on you in the Derby—and you know I only bet on a sure thing." His hand reached out to give her shoulder a fervent squeeze.

At eleven A.M., two men wearing khaki security uniforms drove a gold sedan through to the valet parking area. They were waved through by the guard and parked their car at the jockey's parking zone. They made their way to the main track area by crossing through the receiving barn. There, they split up.

Alix placed second in the first two races with horses who had never been in the money before. Then she won the next two. After every race, Connor was there, tall and expressionless, ready to walk her back to the jockey's room where she would change her silks for the next ride and get rid of as much mud as possible in the few minutes allotted.

Finally, it was time for the eighth race of the day, the Derby, a five-hundred-thousand-dollar purse. She would be up on Pride with a good chance to win, but they'd drawn first gate in the lottery for post position. Pride didn't like being bunched up against the rail by the other horses.

A shiver took her, and she told herself again, as she had so many times that day, that the track itself was probably the safest place for her. After all, there were nearly fifty thousand people there. She came out of the women's jockey room and her gaze went first to Connor. She found him waiting next to the entry, his arms crossed over his chest.

Connor had watched her through the day, race after race, his admiration for her courage and ability growing with each ride. And yes, he finally admitted to himself, he loved her. He loved her open, giving heart, her courage, her sweet vulnerability, and her very real talent. He loved the way she made him feel, the way she teased him and kept him from taking life too seriously. And he had no reason to hide the fact that he loved the effect she had on his body. She staggered him with a look. Of course, they would have to work out something about her money, tie it up in a trust or some such thing. There would be no misconceptions about why he wanted her.

He had learned from Dani that no woman had ever won this Derby before. He wanted it for Alix. He wanted her to be the first, and he wanted her to know that she took his heart with her.

As she crossed the few steps that separated them, he leaned down as if to make a casual comment to her. "Do ye know how I love ye, ye wee witch?" he whispered.

Her hands came up to grab his arms, and her head bent back so that she could see his eyes. He bent to her ear once more and murmured,

"Take care, m'sweetheart . . . and ride with the wind! I've a fancy t'have a Derby winner in the family."

Her lips made a startled "oh" that he wanted to kiss so badly, he had to look away from her. There in the saddling paddock they were surrounded by a multitude—trainers, handlers, jockeys, horses. Alix forgot them all to gaze into her lover's face. When his eyes returned to hers, he saw the answers he would have. But Charlie Wallingham, owner of Pride, was already closing the distance between them. Her hands dropped reluctantly from his arms and she turned.

The older man smiled at her and asked, "How do you feel, Alix?"

"Good, Charlie." She grinned back at him. "Like we're going to win this one." Charlie had been introduced to both Connor and Turk that morning, and he and Connor acknowledged each other with a nod.

Together, the three walked over to the stall where Pride was being saddled. Alix stroked Pride's "sweet spot" and blew her scent into his nostrils. After another pat on the neck, she turned and started the parade to the walking ring, where the spectators would have a good look at both horses and jockeys. Connor stayed only as far from her as the wooden rail. His eyes never stopped moving.

"You know what to do with him, Alix," Charlie told her in an unusual vote of confidence as he patted her back. "He runs better for you than any rider he's ever had. We've gotten this far. Let's show them what he can do." Then he threw her up on Pride's back.

Again, Connor was right beside her. She was so grateful that Turk and he had consented to wear police-issue vests under their clothes. Just knowing they were protected made it easier for her to concentrate on her job.

The rain had stopped. Turk watched Connor walk with Alix and Wallingham from the saddling barn to the walking ring. He was careful to keep his distance, alert to anyone who might be paying them undue attention. Maybe this Bentley character was smarter than they thought. Or maybe he was just biding his time.

Canvassing the area, Turk caught sight of Dani. She was assigned as ponygirl for Alix. Turk had bullied her into wearing a vest as well. He took a moment to admire the way she sat her mount before he followed them through the tunnel that led to the track. They should be safe now until they were off the track. He watched Dani attach her lead to Alix's horse.

As Alix rode in the prerace parade with Dani, she called out, "Everything look okay to you?"

Dani grinned back at her. "No sign of the bad guys."

"Good." Finally, Alix felt free to devote all of her attention to Pride and this, his most important race. "Slow up a little," she told Dani. "I want him anxious." Dani immediately complied, pulling short on the lead until Pride slowed to a fast walk.

Alix decided they had two chances. If Pride had a great start out of the gate, she could take the lead. If he was slow getting out, she could "rate" him, holding him back for an opening. "Sitting chilly," they called it, and it was Alix's specialty. Mud was the problem. Pride didn't mind it much, but she only had four pairs of goggles and the black stuff would be flying if she didn't take the lead.

The three year olds were being put into the gate, and the number two horse was fractious, twisting his neck as he bucked in rebellion. She didn't like him acting up right next to Pride, but her gelding was holding steady.

"That's my boy," she murmured as she took

her grip on his mane. Then for luck, mindful of her man, she said, "That's my bonnie laddie."

They were in position now. The only sounds were last minute commands and the rustlings of bridle and harness, stamping hooves. The air was charged with anticipation and, finally, the bell went off.

With a great leap, Pride was second out of the gate! No choice now. If she didn't go early, the other horses would crowd her against the rail. The rain had begun again, and the mud was a black wind. Changing goggles, she stayed right behind the lead horse. At last, they were around the final turn and into the stretch. Then it happened. Gary Harden was in the lead with Bonds of Love. Gary asked his horse for speed and moved him out, away from the rail. Alix knew he didn't see her behind him, but a hole was opened and Pride sailed right through it. A tidal-wave roar came up from the crowd as Alix pulled ahead by a length . . . two . . . then three. Another two seconds and they were under the wire.

Alix threw her head back and laughed joyously. She stood up in the irons, heart pounding, and sent her fists high in victory!

*   *   *

Connor grabbed her as soon as she reached the winner's circle. His great arms surrounded her, warming her against the cool lash of the rain. "Ye won, m'bonnie! Ye won!" He crowed with triumph against her muddy cheek.

Dani was there, too, ready with a hug and a towel for her face. Then Sammy, careless of the muddy imprint she left upon his precious suit.

"I've been here before," she said happily, looking around the winner's circle, "but it's never felt quite like this! Did you see him?" She grinned at Charlie. "Wasn't he incredible?"

Charlie actually had tears in his eyes. "Couple of thoroughbreds," he said as he nodded. "Now get back up there and get your picture taken. I'm going to make sure it's plastered in every paper from here to Saratoga."

Adrenaline raced through Alix's bloodstream as she and Connor left the winner's circle. There had been so many photographs and congratulations that she was glad she wasn't riding the ninth race. The parade had already begun when they got back to the jockey room. All Alix could think about now was that hot shower waiting for her. She saw Turk at the mouth of the tunnel. He looked pretty menacing.

"Dani's right," Alix said to Connor as they moved through the crowd. She signed autographs like a pro, only slowing, never stopping. "Turk does look like a crook."

"Good." That was just the way Connor wanted it.

"I'll be out in fifteen," she said when they reached the women's jockey room, guarded by a heavyset guard with glasses. "Twenty at most." Connor nodded, his eyes taking in the two roving plainclothes security men. "Then," she whispered, so that only he could hear, "maybe we can find a place where you can tell me again . . . what you said before?"

His expression didn't change, but Alix recognized the light in his eyes. It promised all sorts of wonderful things. But first, she thought, she wanted out of this mud skin. With a shy wave, she headed for the shower.

Turk watched Alix go into the jockey's room, watched Connor station himself right outside.

Listening to the announcer call the finish

of the last race, Turk looked down the tunnel. He watched the crowd as they started to leave, pouring through the concrete pedestrian side. He saw Dani, still on her horse, talking to another ponygirl on the dirt side.

He checked left, then right. He didn't much care for the look of one heavyset man, until the man was joined by his wife and child. When he looked into the tunnel again, he saw Dani's horse, reins dragging. Moving quickly through the flowing crowd, he stepped onto the dirt and ran up to the girl he had seen Dani speaking with.

"Where's Dani?" he asked gruffly.

The girl looked surprised at the question, but she answered, "A security guy came up, asked her to follow him." She gestured to the horse. "I told her I'd get Erin back to the stables. What's up?"

He didn't waste a second more. Darting through the crowd with incredible speed, he searched the stands for Dani's electric blue jacket.

The sound of his beeper made Connor jump away from the wall and curse in annoyance. He looked at the potbellied guard on the other side of the archway, then at the phone on the wall beside the man.

"Can I use that?" he asked, hand on his beeper. "I'm a doctor."

"Sorry," the guard answered. "No outside lines. Phones are that way, near the grandstand, behind the first-aid station." He waved in an airy motion.

Connor gave a short huff of frustration and said, "Okay, look, can you stay here till I get back? I mean right here?"

"Yeah, sure," the guard answered, adjusting his thick glasses. He watched the big man hurry on his way and smiled. Then he took off his glasses and tucked them carefully into his shirt pocket. With a last glance over his shoulder, he turned and went into the jockey's room.

When Connor reached the place Turk had been stationed, there was no sign of him. That's when the hair on the back of Connor's neck began to prickle.

Helmet off, Alix had started to undress as soon as she was inside the locker room door. The mud was drying and it was itchy. The black stuff was even in her hair. She released her hair from its clip and looked around for the valet, before she realized he was probably in the TV room, watching the ninth race. So she laid her clothes and the canister Turk had given her on the bench near her locker.

Her boots were the hardest to get off without help, for they were covered with mud and quite slippery. When she was down to her underwear, she sighed and reached into her locker for her shampoo. That's when she heard the subtle scrape of a footstep behind her. Her head jerked up and, so quickly, a hard arm came around her neck, strangling her.

TEN

Alix froze.

"What you feel under your chin is a knife, dear girl," a voice whispered close to her ear. She could feel the warm moisture of his breath on her neck. "A very sharp, very shiny knife."

Her heart found her throat and lodged there. It had happened. The evil was here.

"How did you find me, Bentley?" she asked calmly, though she felt faint.

"Oh, they have all kinds of computers now, Cat," he told her in a soft, measured voice that chilled her spine. "They can take the picture of a fifteen-year-old and age it as much as you want. They can send that picture anywhere in the world. It didn't take long to track you down." His voice became silky, the way she remembered it sounding when something pleased him. "I gave them your birthday picture. Remember that birthday, Cat? That was the night I had you. Remember? You screeched like a frightened rabbit. 'Eeee, eee!'" He shrilled in imitation. Then he laughed.

Alix gave a tiny jerk of her head—away, *away!*—until she felt the prick of his knife under her chin. His other hand grasped her savagely around the ribs, cutting off her air supply. *Don't panic*, she told herself. *Stay calm.* They'll come soon. Someone will come. But another part of her mind was screaming that she would die before she let Bentley rape her again.

His fingers moved toward her breast in caressing motions as he murmured, "I've already killed a man, you know. I did it with this knife." A tiny gasp of horror escaped her. "I didn't even mind the blood." His voice changed again, to something cold, ugly. "That sniveling little computer detective I hired to find you got greedy. He thought he could get money from you and blackmail me too. But, I showed him what happens to those who try to cross me." Bentley made a strange, giggling sound. "No one even knows. It's amazing how easy it was, Cat. I was really quite surprised."

Alix tried to quiet her runaway heartbeat. He smelled of expensive cologne and something almost metallic. She wondered briefly if she was going to be sick.

"I've told the police about you, Bentley. They know about the trust, the accidents. They know you have a motive to get rid of me."

"Just circumstantial evidence, little cat. They'll never prove I was here. You passed me without a second look." He pressed the soft cushion of his fake paunch into her back. "I walked right up to the guard and a trainer, and informed the guard they needed him in the stable area. All it took was the name of his boss. They were betting on you to win, Cat. Did you win?" When she didn't immediately answer, he let his hand cover her breast and squeezed. "Hmm?"

"Yes!" She twisted, not caring that the sharp blade pricked her skin again. This time she could feel the warm liquid of her own blood slip down the front of her throat. But she wasn't ready to make her move, not until his knife hand was somewhere she might be able to grab it.

"They're gone now, Cat . . . all gone." His hot breath touched her cheek, and with his next words, her blood ran cold in her veins. "So is your big doctor."

"What did you say?" she croaked out.

"I've taken care of your lover. Did you think I would let him stop me? No, it'll all be over by the time he finds you."

"What did you do, Bentley?" she asked in a shaky voice. She could feel by the change in his body tension that he liked frightening her.

"I simply made sure I'd have you all to myself, little cat."

She felt the cold, wet swipe of his tongue at her neck and, masking her revulsion, she went over Turk's lessons in her mind. With her next breath, she pressed her body back against his, away from the knife. *What if something had really happened to Connor? And where was Turk?*

"You're going to slip in the shower," Bentley went on. "Terrible accident. Unless, of course, you force me to slit your throat. But that would make for such a mess, don't you think?" He sighed. "It's too bad we don't really have time for more fun and games. You still look like a boy . . ." He leaned down and whispered, "But I did so like the way you squirmed under me . . ."

Now. This was her chance! Jerking back against him with all her might, Alix threw him off balance against the bench. Grabbing his knife hand, she kept her own balance with it as she twisted and gave his groin the kick of her life. Then, just as she felt the impact, she let go of his hand. His arms waved wildly as he tried to stay on his feet, but he landed flat on his back, ankles draped over the bench. And he was moaning.

Music to her ears.

Alix wasted no time. She grabbed the small canister from the bench where her silks lay and sprayed Bentley right in the eyes. He screamed in outrage as the green foam exploded, masking his face in three thick inches of lather. He slashed at the empty air with his knife as his other hand rubbed at the thick foam.

Alix heard running footsteps behind her and whirled around in a crouch, but the man who came through the door was Connor. With a low sob, she launched herself into the safety of his arms. He gave her a reassuring hug, then put her from him with a murderous growl at the sight of the blood on her throat.

She could only watch in amazement as Connor snatched Bentley up from the floor like a wet rag and shook him. He twisted her cousin's wrist until she heard a horrible cracking sound and the knife fell to the floor. Then her gentle Scot began to pummel Bentley with blows to his face and ribs until Turk came rushing in and pulled them apart.

Panting in furious breaths, Connor turned back to Alix. His hands curled into great green fists. She let go a tiny, hysterical giggle at the sight, and he raised his arms. She ran to him, burying her face in his warm neck as his hands clutched at her back.

She learned from the conversation she over-heard between Turk and Connor that Turk had found Dani bound and gagged in a bathroom. By then he'd known he'd been diverted on purpose, just as Connor had known when Turk wasn't where they'd agreed he would stay. Dani was fine, though she was pretty angry about being left on the grandstand steps with her hands and feet still tied.

Bentley was green and raving when the police finally took him away. Alix told them about the murder Bentley had confessed to, then she endured hugs from Sammy and Dani and whoever reached for her. She never did get her shower.

When she started to shake with reaction, Connor bundled her into a blanket and carried her to his car despite her protests. She finally realized he was right, for once they were on their way home, a strange exhaustion joined her helpless quakes as she huddled against the window.

Connor realized Alix was experiencing more than simple physical reaction. He'd seen it before. A psychological effect tagged along with violent crime, especially when the assailant was known to the victim. In this case, because Bentley was a relative, there would probably be misplaced guilt and helpless rage in equal measures. The only real remedies he knew for those psychological effects were warmth, caring, and sleep.

By the time he pulled into his driveway, her teeth were chattering. He came around to her door and lifted her into his arms. Her own arms went around his neck. He stood there, unable to move. She was so precious to him, and for a moment he was filled with simple awe that she was safe and in his arms.

"I love you, Connor," she whispered between quakes.

"Och, sweetheart," he said huskily. "Ye tear me apart."

He turned and marched to his front door. As soon as they were inside, he stalked through to the master bath and put her down inside the tub. He pulled the blanket away, leaving her in her sleeveless T-shirt and panties.

Alix watched from what seemed like a great distance as he turned on the water, poured in bubble bath, and peeled away her wet underthings. Suddenly, she giggled, then giggled again as he frowned down at her. "Your hands . . ." She stared at the red scrapes and green color that stained his knuckles.

"It doesna wash away," he told her, looking displeased.

"I know." She reached for one hand and pressed her lips to the strange design. That tattoo would last seven days, and each day she would be reminded that because of love for her, a gentle man had become a fierce protector. "I have a confession to make."

"Aye, lassie?" Connor turned his hand so that his palm cupped her cheek. Tremors still shook her. "Let me get something to help ye sleep a bit."

"No drugs," she murmured. "But I wouldn't mind some of your whisky."

"Fine." He went to get her drink. When he returned, she was staring into the bubbles. He knelt down to put the glass to her lips. "Sip," he ordered. She did, and the alcohol warmed her insides as the water warmed the rest of her.

"Now." Connor placed the glass on the side of the tub and reached for the soap. "What is this latest confession?" He rinsed the blood from the cut under her chin as if she were five years old. Then he turned her so that he could reach her shoulders. With long, slow strokes, he began to knead the tension from her muscles.

"You know when you came bursting into the locker room?" she asked shyly, head down.

"Aye." His fingers sliding over the nape of her neck, way up, way down.

"And then you grabbed Bentley and started pounding him?"

He growled in remembered satisfaction.

"It was like . . ." She bent her head to one side and closed her eyes. "Like a fairy-tale rescue I'd always waited for." His hands stilled. "I mean . . . when I gave him that kick . . . it felt *so* good! As if I had won a battle against an enemy I'd fought all my life!" His fingers moved again, slowly, caressingly. "But when you came crashing through that door, when I saw the rage on your face that someone would dare try to hurt me . . . Connor, I fell in love with you all over again."

With her last words, he twisted her around enough so he could kiss her honeyed mouth. "You're mine, sweetheart," he said between luscious kisses. "An' I love ye true."

Alix turned all the way around, careless of the fact that her arms were drenching him. They rocked together for a long time, until Connor's hands began to glide over her. He reached for the soap once more.

"He's insane, isn't he?" she said thoughtfully, watching him roll the soap between his hands in sensuous motions.

"Aye, love."

"Strange that knowing that would make me feel better, but it does."

Connor handed her back the glass of whisky, and she offered him a sip. Eyes to hers, he took it. Then he soaped her arms, her breasts, her belly, and below. He was trying to maintain a medical distance, but the feel of her silky flesh under his hands was devastating to his senses. When she began to move against his hand, he stopped all motion, trying to remember that she was still somewhat in shock.

"Connor?" Her voice was a ragged whisper. Her hands had risen to grasp the sides of the tub. "Are you going to marry me?"

"Aye, that I am," he said definitively. Putting the soap carefully in the dish, he began to rinse the bubbles away from her shoulders. He watched the rivulets flow over her collarbone, watched them shape her breasts and belly.

"Truly?" she asked, her eyes closed in dreamy contemplation.

"Aye, sweetheart." He was puzzled. What was going through her mind now?

"Then, my love." She laughed and leaned over to nip at the corner of his mouth. "My big braw Scot . . . I think you had better start learning to tell when it's time to make love to me."

His eyes met hers, and he reached up to paint her lower lip with one damp finger. Then his hand moved to his tie and pulled downward until it fell from about his neck. "Aye, sweetheart." His voice was the low grumble she loved. "But it may take a wee bit o' practice. I can be a slow learner, ye ken."

Her grin filled his heart as her hands lifted to his shirt.

"Until you get it right, Doc. Until you get it right."

THE EDITOR'S
CORNER

July belongs to ONLY DADDY—and six magnificent heroes who discover romance, family style! Whether he's a confirmed bachelor or a single father, a small-town farmer or a big-city cop, each of these men can't resist the pitter-patter of little feet. And when he falls under the spell of that special woman's charms, he'll stop at nothing to claim her as a partner in parenting and passion. . . .

Leading the terrific line-up for July is Linda Cajio with **ME AND MRS. JONES**, LOVESWEPT #624. Actually, it should be *ex-*Mrs. Jones since high school sweethearts Kate Perry and Mitch Jones have been divorced for eleven years, after an elopement and a disastrous brief marriage. Now Kate is back in town, and Mitch, who's always been able to talk her into just about anything, persuades her to adopt a wise-eyed injured tomcat, with the promise that he'd be making plenty of house calls! Not sure she can play stepmother to his daughter Chelsea, Kate tells herself to run from the man who so easily ignites her desire, but she still remembers his hands on her body and can't send him away. To Mitch, no memory can ever match the heat of their passion, and he's been waiting all this time to reclaim the only woman he's ever truly loved. With fire in his touch, he sets about convincing her to let him in once more, and this time he intends to keep her in his arms for always. An utterly delightful story from beginning to end, told with Linda's delicious sense of humor and sensitive touch.

In **RAISING HARRY**, LOVESWEPT #625 by Victoria Leigh, Griff Ross is a single father coping with the usual problems of raising a high-spirited three-year-old son. He's never been jealous of Harry until he finds him in the arms of their neighbor Sharron Capwell. Her lush mouth makes Griff long to kiss her breathless, while her soft curves tempt him with visions of bare shoulders touched only by moonlight and his hands. She makes him burn with pleasure as no woman ever has, but Griff, still hurt by a betrayal he's never forgiven, insists he wants only a friend and a lover. Single and childless, Sharron has always been content with her life—until she thrills to the ecstacy Griff shows her, and now finds herself struggling with her need to be his wife and Harry's mother. Rest assured that a happily-ever-after awaits these two, as well as the young one, once they admit the love they can't deny. Victoria tells a compelling love story, one you won't be able to put down.

Who can resist **THE COURTING COWBOY**, LOVESWEPT #626 by Glenna McReynolds? Ty Garrett is a rough-edged rancher who wants a woman to share the seasons, to love under the Colorado skies. But he expects that finding a lady in his middle-of-nowhere town would be very rough—until a spirited visiting teacher fascinates his son and captivates him too! Victoria Willoughby has beautiful skin, a very kissable mouth, and a sensual innocence that beckons Ty to woo her with fierce, possessive passion. He awakens her to pleasures she's never imagined, teaches her how wonderful taking chances can be, and makes her feel alluring, wanton. But she's already let one man rule her life and she's vowed never to belong to anyone ever again. Still, she knows that finding Ty is a miracle; now if she'll only realize that he's the best man and the right man for her . . . Glenna's talent shines brightly in this terrific romance.

Bonnie Pega begins her deliciously sexy novel, **THEN COMES MARRIAGE**, LOVESWEPT #627, with the hero and heroine meeting in a very unlikely place. Single mother-to-be Libby Austin certainly thinks that seeing the hunk of her dreams in a childbirth class is truly rotten luck, but she breathes a sigh of relief when she discovers that Zac Webster is coaching his sister-in-law, not his wife! His potent masculinity can charm every stitch of clothing off a woman's body; too bad he makes it all too clear that a child doesn't fit into his life. Still, unable to resist the temptation of Libby's blue velvet eyes and delectable smile, Zac lays siege to her senses, and her response of torrential kisses and fevered caresses drive him even wilder with hunger. Libby has given him more than he's hoped for—and a tricky dilemma. Can a man who's sworn off marriage and vows he's awful with kids claim a wildfire bride and her baby? With this wonderful romance, her second LOVESWEPT, Bonnie proves that she's a name to watch for.

There's no sexier **MAN AROUND THE HOUSE** than the hero in Cindy Gerard's upcoming LOVESWEPT, #628. Matthew Spencer is a lean, muscled heartbreaker, and when he answers his new next-door neighbor's cries for help, he finds himself rescuing disaster-prone Katie

McDonald, who's an accident waiting to happen—and a sassy temptress who's sure to keep him up nights. Awakening his hunger with the speed of a summer storm, Katie senses his pain and longs to comfort him, but Matthew makes her feel too much, makes her want more than she can have. Though she lets herself dare to dream of being loved, Katie knows she's all wrong for a man who's walking a careful path to regain custody of his son. He needs nice and normal, not her kind of wild and reckless—no matter that they sizzle in each other's arms. But Matthew's not about to give up a woman who adores his child, listens to his favorite golden oldie rock station, and gives him kisses that knock his socks off and make the stars spin. The magic of Cindy's writing shines through in this enchanting tale of love.

Finishing the line-up in a big way is Marcia Evanick and **IN DADDY'S ARMS**, LOVESWEPT #629. Brave enough to fight back from wounds inflicted in the line of duty, Bain O'Neill is devastated when doctors tell him he'll never be a father. Having a family is the only dream that ever mattered to him, a fantasy he can't give up, not when he knows that somewhere there are two children who are partly his, the result of an anonymous sperm donation he made years ago. A little investigation helps him locate his daughters—and their mother, Erin Flynn, a fiery-haired angel who tastes as good as she looks. Widowed for two years, Erin takes his breath away and heals him with her loving touch. Bain hates keeping the truth from her, and though the children soon beg him to be their daddy, he doesn't dare confess his secret to Erin, not until he's silenced her doubts about his love and makes her believe he's with her to stay forever. All the stirring emotions and funny touches that you've come to expect from Marcia are in this fabulous story.

On sale this month from Bantam are three spectacular women's novels. Dianne Edouard and Sandra Ware have teamed up once again and written **SACRED LIES,** a spellbinding novel of sin, seduction, and betrayal. Romany Chase is the perfect spy: intelligent, beautiful, a woman who thrills to the hunt. But with her latest mission, Romany is out of her depth. Adrift in a world where redemption may arrive too late, she is torn between the enigmatic priest she has orders to seduce and the fierce agent she desires. Beneath the glittering Roman moon, a deadly conspiracy of greed, corruption, and shattering evil is closing in, and Romany must choose whom to believe—and whom to love.

With more than several million copies of her novels in print, Kay Hooper is indisputably one of the best loved and popular authors of romantic fiction—and now she has penned **THE WIZARD OF SEATTLE,** a fabulous, magical story of immortal love and mesmerizing fantasy. Serena Smyth travels cross-country to Seattle to find Richard Patrick Merlin, guided by an instinct born of her determination to become a master wizard like him. She knows he can be her teacher, but she never expects the fire he ignites in her body and soul. Their love forbidden by an ancient law, Serena and Merlin will take a desperate gamble and travel to the long-lost world of Atlantis—to change the history that threatens to keep them apart for eternity.

From bestselling author Susan Johnson comes **SILVER FLAME,** the steamy sequel about the Braddock-Black dynasty you read about in **BLAZE.** Pick up a copy and find out why *Romantic Times* gave the author its Best Sensual Historical Romance Award. Sizzling with electrifying sensuality, **SILVER FLAME** burns hot! When Empress

Jordan is forced to sell her most precious possession to the highest bidder in order to feed her brothers and sisters, Trey Braddock-Black knows he must have her, no matter what the cost. The half-Absarokee rogue has no intention of settling down with one woman, but once he's spent three weeks with the sweet enchantress, he knows he can never give her up. . . .

Also on sale this month, in the hardcover edition from Doubleday, is **THE PAINTED LADY,** the stunningly sensual debut novel by Lucia Grahame. All of Paris and London recognize Fleur not only as Frederick Brooks's wife, but also as the successful painter's most inspiring model. But few know the secrets behind his untimely death and the terrible betrayal that leaves Fleur with a heart of ice—and no choice but to accept Sir Anthony Camwell's stunning offer: a fortune to live on in return for five nights of unrestrained surrender to what he plans to teach her—the exquisite art of love.

Happy reading!

With warmest wishes,

Nita Taublib

Nita Taublib
Associate Publisher
LOVESWEPT and FANFARE

Don't miss these exciting
books by your favorite
Bantam authors
On Sale in May:

SACRED LIES
by Dianne Edouard
and Sandra Ware

THE WIZARD OF SEATTLE
by Kay Hooper

SILVER FLAME
by Susan Johnson

SACRED LIES
by Dianne Edouard and Sandra Ware

On Sale in May

Romany Chase is the perfect spy: intelligent, beautiful, a woman who thrills to the hunt. But torn between the fierce Israeli agent she desires and the enigmatic priest she has orders to seduce, Romany is out of her depth—adrift in a world where redemption may arrive too late . . . .

As soon as Romany opened the door, she knew she wasn't alone. Someone waited for her. Somewhere in the apartment.

She had never carried a gun. There had never been a need. Even though Sully could have gotten her easy clearance, and had more than once urged her to take along some insurance. But her assignments never warranted it. Except that one time, in Geneva, and that situation had come totally out of left field.

She allowed her eyes to become adjusted to the gloom and, easing herself against the wall, moved to the edge of the living room. She searched the shadows. Strained to see something behind the thick lumps and bumps of furniture. Nothing. She crouched lower and inched closer to the door opening into her bedroom.

She peered around the corner. Whoever was in the apartment had switched on the ceiling fan and the small lamp that sat on a dressing table in the adjoining bath. The soft light cast the room in semidarkness, and she could make out the large solid shape of a man. He reclined easily upon her bed, a marshmallowy heap of pillows propped against his back. He hadn't bothered to draw back the covers, and he lay on top of the spread completely naked.

She should have run, gotten out of her apartment as quickly as possible. Except she recognized the hard muscles under the deeply tanned skin, the black curling hair, the famous smirk that passed for a smile. Recognized the man who was a cold-blooded killer—and her lover.

Romany moved through the doorway and smiled. "I'm not even going to ask how you got in here, David."

She heard his dark laugh. "Is that any way to greet an old friend?"

She walked farther into the room and stood by the side of the bed. She stared into the bright green eyes, still a surprise after all this time. But then everything about David ben Haar was a surprise. "Why don't you make yourself comfortable?"

"I am . . . almost." He reached for her hand and ran it slowly down his chest, stopping just short of the black hair at his groin.

She glanced down, focusing on her hand, pale and thin clasped inside his. She could hear her breath catch inside her throat. And as if that sound had been meant as some sort of signal, he pulled her down beside him.

She rested with her back against him, letting him work the muscles at her shoulders, brush his lips against her hair. She didn't turn when she finally decided to speak. "What are you doing here, David?"

"I came to see you." The words didn't sound like a complete lie.

She twisted herself round to look up at him. "That's terribly flattering, David, but it won't work."

She watched the smirk almost stretch into a real smile.

"Okay, I came to make sure that Sully is taking good care of my girl."

"I'm not your girl, David." She tried not to sound mean, or hurt, or anything. But she could feel the muscles of his stomach tighten against her back.

"You know Sully's a fucking asshole," he said finally. "What's he waiting on, those jerks to open up a concentration camp and gas a few thousand Jews?"

"David, Sully's not an asshole. . . . Hey, what in the hell do you mean?" She jerked around, waiting for an answer, watching his eyes turn cold.

"Gimme a break, Romany."

"Dammit, David, I don't have the slightest idea what you're talking about. Besides, what in the hell have concentration camps got to do with . . . ?" She stopped short, not willing to play her hand, even though David probably knew all the cards she was holding.

"Well, Romany, I can save you, and Sully, and all your little friends over at the CIA a whole helluva lotta trouble. Somebody—and I think you're deaf, dumb, and blind if you haven't pegged who that is—is stealing the Church blind, swiping paintings right off the museum walls, then slipping by some pretty goddamn good fakes."

She watched him stare at her from inside the darkness of her bed, waiting with that flirting smirk on his mouth for her to say something. But she didn't answer.

" . . . And the SOB at the other end of this operation"—he was finishing what he'd started—"whether your CIA geniuses want to admit it or not, is black-marketing the genuine articles, funneling the profits to a group of neo-Nazis who aren't going to settle for German reunification."

"Neo-Nazis?"

She could hear him grit his teeth. "Yeah, neo-Nazis. Getting East and West Germany together was just the first stage of their nasty little operation. They've got big plans, Romany. But they're the same old fuckers. Just a little slicker."

"David, I can't believe—"

"Shit, you people never want to believe—"

"Stop it, David."

He dropped his head and took in a deep staccatoed breath. She felt his hands move up her arms to her shoulders and force her body close to his. "Sorry, Romany." He sounded hoarse. Then suddenly she felt him laughing against her. "You know something"—he was drawing back—"you're on the wrong side, Romany. We wouldn't have these stupid fights if you'd come and work with me. With the Mossad."

"Yeah? Work with you, huh? And just what inducement can you offer, David ben Haar?" She pulled away from him and stood up.

Her feelings about David were a tangled mess—which, after she'd watched him board the plane for Tel Aviv thirteen months ago, she'd thought she could safely leave unwound. But here he was again, still looking at her with that quizzical twist to his lips that she couldn't help but read as a challenge.

She wanted his hands on her. That was the thought that kept repeating itself, blotting out everything else in her mind. Her own hands trembled as she pushed the hair away from her neck and began to undo the buttons at her back. Undressing for him slowly, the way he liked it.

She hadn't let herself know how much she'd missed this, until she was beneath the covers naked beside him, and his hands were really on her again, taking control, his mouth moving everywhere on her body. The pulse of the ceiling fan blended suddenly with the rush of blood in her ears, and David's heat was under her skin like fire.

She pressed herself closer against him, her need for him blocking out her doubts. She wanted his solidness, his back under her hands, the hardness of him along the length of her body. David ben Haar, the perfect sexual fantasy. But real. Flesh and blood with eyes green as the sea. She looked into his eyes as he pulled her beneath him. There was no lightness in them now, only the same intensity of passion as when he killed. He came into her hard, and she shut her eyes, matching her rhythm to his. To dream was all right, as long as you didn't let it go beyond the borders of your bed.

* * *

With one small edge of the curtain rolled back, David ben Haar could just see through the balcony railing where the red Alfa Romeo Spider was waiting to park in the street. Romany had been flying about the apartment when the car had first driven up, still cursing him for her half-damp hair, amusingly anxious to keep the priest from getting as far as her door.

"I could hide in the bedroom." He had said it from his comfortable position, lying still naked on her sofa. Laughing at her as she went past buttoning her dress, hobbling on one shoe back to the bedroom.

"I don't trust you, David ben Haar." She'd come back with her other shoe and was throwing a hairbrush into that satchel she called a purse.

"Romany?" He had concentrated on the intent face, the wild curls threatening to break loose from the scarf that bound them. "Morrow one of the bad guys?"

Picking up a sweater, she had looked over at him then, with something remarkably like guilt. "I don't know." She was going for the door. "That's what I'm supposed to find out."

Then she was gone, her heels rat-tatting down the stairs. High heels at Villa d'Este. Just like an American. They never took anything seriously, then covered it up with a cynicism they hadn't earned. Romany was the flip side of that, of course, all earnestness and innocence. She was smart and she had guts. But it wouldn't be enough to protect her. He got up.

As he watched now, the Spider was swinging into the parking space that had finally become available at the curb. The door opened and a man got out, turning to where Romany had just emerged from under the balcony overhang. The man didn't exactly match the car, he looked far too American. What he didn't look like was a priest.

He watched them greet each other. Very friendly. The compressor on the air conditioner picked that minute to kick in again, so he couldn't hope to hear what was said. The man opened the passenger door for her, then walked around to get in. They didn't pull out right away, and he was wondering why when he saw the canvas top go down. The engine roared up as they shot away from the curb. He could tell by the tilt of her head that Romany was laughing.

They had not spoken for some time now, standing among the tall cypress, looking out below to the valley. The dying sun had painted everything in a kind of saturated light, and he seemed almost surreal standing next to her, his fair aureole of hair and tall body in light-colored shirt and slacks glowing against the blackness of the trees.

They had played today, she and Julian Morrow. Like happy strangers who had met in Rome, with no history and no future. She had felt it immediately, the playfulness, implicit in the red car, in the way he wore the light, casual clothes. Like an emblem, like a costume at a party.

She had sat in the red car, letting the wind blow everything away from her mind, letting it rip David from her body. Forgetting the job. Forgetting that the man beside her was a priest and a suspect, and she a paid agent of the United States government.

They had played today. And she had liked this uncomplicated persona better than any he had so far let her see. Liked his ease and his sense of humor, and the pleasure he had seemed to find in their joyful sharing of this place. She had to stop playing now, but this was the Julian Morrow she must hold in her mind. Not the priest. Not the suspect in criminal forgery. But a Julian Morrow to whom she could want to make love.

He turned to her and smiled. For a moment the truth of her treachery rose to stick in her throat. But she forced it down. This was her job. She was committed.

She smiled back, moving closer, as if she might want a better view, or perhaps some little shelter from the wind. He must have thought the latter, because she felt his hands draping her sweater more firmly around her shoulders.

Time to take the advantage. And shifting backward, she pressed herself lightly against his chest, her eyes closed. She was barely breathing, feeling for any answering strain. But she could find no sense of any rejection in his posture.

She turned. He was looking down at her. His eyes, so close, were unreadable. She would never remember exactly what had happened next, but she knew when her arms went around him. And the small moment of her triumph when she felt him hard against her. Then she was pulling him down toward her, her fingers tangling in his hair, her mouth moving on his.

At the moment when she ceased thinking at all, he let her go, suddenly, with a gesture almost brutal that set her tumbling back. His hand reached for her wrist, didn't let her fall. But the grip was not kind or gentle.

His face was closed. Completely. Anger would have been better. She was glad when he turned away from her, walking back in the direction of the car. There would be no dinner tonight at the wonderful terraced restaurant he had talked about today. Of that she was perfectly sure. It was going to be a long drive back to Rome.

THE WIZARD OF SEATTLE
the unique new romantic fantasy from Kay Hooper

On Sale in May

In the bestselling tradition of the time-travel romances of Diana Gabaldon and Constance O'Day-Flannery, Kay Hooper creates her own fabulous, magical story of timeless love and mesmerizing fantasy.

She looked like a ragged, storm-drenched urchin, but from the moment Serena Smyth appeared on his Seattle doorstep Richard Patrick Merlin recognized the spark behind her green eyes, the wild talent barely held in check. And he would help her learn to control her gift, despite a taboo so ancient that the reasons for its existence had been forgotten. But he never suspected that in his rebellion he would risk all he had and all he was to feel a love none of his kind had ever known.

Seattle, 1984

It was his home. She knew that, although where her certainty came from was a mystery to her. Like the inner tug that had drawn her across the country to find him, the knowledge seemed instinctive, beyond words or reason. She didn't even know his name. But she knew what he was. He was what she wanted to be, needed to be, what all her instincts insisted she had to be, and only he could teach her what she needed to learn.

Until this moment, she had never doubted that he would accept her as his pupil. At sixteen, she was passing through that stage of development experienced by humans, twice in their lifetimes, a stage marked by total self-absorption and the unshakable certainty that the entire universe revolves around oneself. It occurred in infancy and in adolescence, but rarely ever again, unless one were utterly unconscious of reality. Those traits had given her the confidence she had needed in order to cross the country alone with no more than a ragged backpack and a few dollars.

But they deserted her now, as she stood at the wrought iron gates and stared up at the secluded old Victorian house. The rain beat down on her, and lightning flashed in the stormy sky, illuminating the turrets and gables of the house; there were few lighted windows, and those were dim rather than welcoming.

It *looked* like the home of a wizard.

She almost ran, abruptly conscious of her aloneness. But then she squared her thin shoulders, shoved open the gate, and walked steadily to the front door. Ignoring the bell, she used the brass knocker to rap sharply. The knocker was fashioned in the shape of an owl, the creature that symbolized wisdom, a familiar of wizards throughout fiction.

She didn't know about fact.

Her hand was shaking, and she gave it a fierce frown as she rapped the knocker once more against the solid door. She barely had time to release the knocker before the door was pulled open.

Tall and physically powerful, his raven hair a little shaggy and his black eyes burning with an inner fire, he surveyed the dripping, ragged girl on his doorstep with lofty disdain for long moments during which all of her determination melted away to nothing. Then he caught her collar with one elegant hand, much as he might have grasped a stray cat, and yanked her into the well-lit entrance hall. He studied her with daunting sternness.

What he saw was an almost painfully thin girl who looked much younger than her sixteen years. Her threadbare clothing was soaked; her short, tangled hair was so wet that only a hint of its normal vibrant red color was apparent; and her small face—all angles and seemingly filled with huge eyes—was white and pinched. She was no more attractive than a stray mongrel pup.

"Well?"

The vast poise of sixteen years deserted the girl as he barked the one word in her ear. She gulped. "I—I want to be a wizard," she managed finally, defiantly.

"Why?"

She was soaked to the skin, tired, hungry, and possessed a temper that had more than once gotten her into trouble. Her green eyes snapping, she glared up into his handsome, expressionless face, and her voice lost all its timidity.

"I *will* be a wizard! If you won't teach me, I'll find someone who will. I can summon fire already—a little—and I can *feel* the power inside me. All I need is a teacher, and I'll be great one day—"

He lifted her clear off the floor and shook her briefly, effortlessly, inducing silence with no magic at all. "The first lesson an apprentice must learn," he told her calmly, "is to never—ever—shout at a Master."

Then he casually released her, conjured a bundle of clothing out of thin air, and handed it to her. Then he waved a hand negligently and sent her floating up the dark stairs toward a bathroom.

And so it began.

Seattle, Present

His fingers touched her breasts, stroking soft skin and teasing the hard pink nipples. The swollen weight filled his hands as he lifted and kneaded, and when she moaned and arched her back, he lowered his mouth to her. He stopped thinking.

He felt. He felt his own body, taut and pulsing with desire, the blood hot in his veins. He felt her body, soft and warm and willing. He felt her hand on him, stroking slowly, her touch hungry and assured. Her moans and sighs filled his ears, and the heat of her need rose until her flesh burned. The tension inside him coiled more tightly, making his body ache, until he couldn't stand to wait another moment. He sank his flesh into hers, feeling her legs close strongly about his hips. Expertly, lustfully, she met his thrusts, undulating beneath him, her female body the cradle all men returned to. The heat between them built until it was a fever raging out of control, until his body was gripped by the inescapable, inexorable drive for release and pounded frantically inside her. Then, at last, the heat and tension drained from him in a rush . . .

Serena sat bolt upright in bed, gasping. In shock, she stared across the darkened room for a moment, and then she hurriedly leaned over and turned on the lamp on the nightstand. Blinking in the light, she held her hands up and stared at them, reassuring herself that they were hers, still slender and pale and tipped with neat oval nails.

They were hers. She was here and unchanged. Awake. Aware. Herself again.

She could still feel the alien sensations, still see the powerful bronzed hands against paler, softer skin, and still feel sensations her body was incapable of experiencing simply because she was female, not male—

And then she realized.

"Dear God . . . Richard," she whispered.

She had been inside his mind, somehow, in his head just like before, and he had been with another woman. He had been having sex with another woman. Serena had felt what he felt, from the sensual enjoyment of soft female flesh under his touch to the ultimate draining pleasure of orgasm. *She had felt what he felt.*

She drew her knees up and hugged them, feeling tears burning her eyes and nausea churning in her stomach. Another woman. He had a woman somewhere, and she wasn't new because there had been a sense of familiarity in him, a certain knowledge. He knew this woman. Her skin was familiar, her taste, her desire. His body knew hers.

Even Master wizards, it seemed, had appetites just like other men.

Serena felt a wave of emotions so powerful she could endure them only in silent anguish. Her thoughts were tangled and fierce and raw. Not a monk, no, hardly a monk. In fact, it appeared he was quite a proficient lover, judging by the woman's response to him.

On her nightstand, the lamp's bulb burst with a violent sound, but she neither heard it nor noticed the return of darkness to the room.

So he was just a man after all, damn him, a man who got horny like other men and went to some woman who'd spread her legs for him. And often. His trips "out of town" were more frequent these last years. Oh, horny indeed . . .

Unnoticed by Serena, her television set flickered to life, madly scanned though all the channels, and then died with a sound as apologetic as a muffled cough.

Damn him. What'd he do, keep a mistress? Some pretty, pampered blonde—she had been blond, naturally—with empty hot eyes who wore slinky nightgowns and crotchless panties, and moaned like a bitch in heat? Was there only one? Or had he bedded a succession of women over the years, keeping his reputation here in Seattle all nice and tidy while he satisfied his appetites elsewhere?

Serena heard a little sound, and was dimly shocked to realize it came from her throat. It sounded like that of an animal in pain, some tortured creature hunkered down in the dark as it waited helplessly to find out if it would live or die. She didn't realize that she was rocking gently. She didn't see her alarm clock flash a series of red numbers before going dark, or notice that her stereo system was spitting out tape from a cassette.

Only when the overhead light suddenly exploded was Serena jarred from her misery. With a tremendous effort, she struggled to control herself.

"Concentrate," she whispered. "Concentrate. Find the switch." And, for the first time, perhaps spurred on by her urgent need to control what she felt, she did find it. Her wayward energies stopped swirling all around her and were instantly drawn into some part of her she'd never recognized before, where they were completely and safely contained, held there in waiting without constant effort from her.

Moving stiffly, feeling exhausted, Serena got out of bed and moved cautiously across the room to her closet, trying to avoid the shards of glass sprinkled over the rugs and the polished wood floor. There were extra lightbulbs on the closet shelf, and she took one to replace the one from her nightstand lamp. It was difficult to unscrew the burst bulb, but she managed; she didn't trust herself to flick all the shattered pieces out of existence with her powers, not when she'd come so close to losing control entirely.

When the lamp was burning again, she got a broom and dustpan and cleaned up all the bits of glass. A slow survey of the room revealed what else she had destroyed, and she shivered a little at the evidence of just how dangerous unfocused power could be.

Ironically, she couldn't repair what she had wrecked, not by using the powers that had destroyed. Because she didn't understand the technology of television or radio or even clocks, it simply wasn't possible for her to focus her powers to fix what was broken. It would be like the blind trying to put together by touch alone something they couldn't even recognize enough to define.

To create or control anything, it was first necessary to understand its very elements, its basic structure, and how it functioned. How many times had Merlin told her that? Twenty times? A hundred?

Serena sat down on her bed, still feeling drained. But not numb; that mercy wasn't granted to her. The switch she had found to contain her energies could do nothing to erase the memory of Richard with another woman.

It hurt. She couldn't believe how much it hurt. All these years she had convinced herself that she was the only woman in his life who mattered, and now she knew that wasn't true. He didn't belong only to her. He didn't belong to her at all. He really didn't see her as a woman—or, if he did, she obviously held absolutely no attraction for him.

The pain was worse, knowing that.

Dawn had lightened the windows by the time Serena tried to go back to sleep. But she couldn't. She lay beneath the covers staring up at the ceiling, feeling older than she had ever felt before. There was no limbo now, no sense of being suspended between woman and child; Serena knew she could never again be a child, not even to protect herself.

The question was—how was that going to alter her relationship with Merlin? Could she pretend there was nothing different? No. Could she even bear to look at him without crying out her pain and rage? Probably not. How would he react when she made her feelings plain, with disgust or pity? That was certainly possible. Would her raw emotion drive him even farther away from her? Or was he, even now, planning to banish her from his life completely?

Because he knew. He knew what she had discovered in the dark watches of the night.

Just before her own shock had wrenched her free of his mind, Serena had felt for a split-second *his* shock as he sensed and recognized her presence intruding on that intensely private act.

He knew. He knew she had been there.

It was another part of her pain, the discomfiting guilt and

shame of having been, however unintentionally, a voyeur. She had a memory now that she would never forget, but it was his, not hers. She'd stolen it from him . . . . And of all the things they both had to face when he came home, that one was likely to be the most difficult of all.

The only certainty Serena could find in any of it was the knowledge that nothing would ever be the same again.

SILVER FLAME
by Susan Johnson

On Sale in May

She was driven by love to break every rule . . . . Empress
Jordan had fled to the Montana wilderness to escape a cruel
injustice, only to find herself forced to desperate means to
feed her brothers and sisters. Once she agreed to sell her most
precious possession to the highest bidder, she feared she'd made
a terrible mistake—even as she found herself hoping it was the
tall, dark, chiseled stranger who had taken her dare and claimed
her . . . .

Empress stood before him, unabashed in her nudity, and
raising her emerald eyes the required height to meet his so
far above, she said "What *will* you do with me, Mr. Braddock-
Black?"

"Trey," he ordered, unconscious of his lightly command-
ing tone.

"What *will* you do with me, Trey?" she repeated correcting
herself as ordered. But there was more than a hint of impudence in her tone and in her tilted mouth and arched brow.

Responding to the impudence with some of his own, he
replied with a small smile, "Whatever you prefer, Empress,
darling." He towered over her, clothed and booted, as dark
as Lucifer, and she was intensely aware of his power and size,
as if his presence seemed to invade her. "You set the pace,
sweetheart," he said encouragingly, reaching out to slide the

pad of one finger slowly across her shoulder. "But take your time," he went on, recognizing his own excitement, running his warm palm up her neck and cupping the back of her head lightly. Trey's voice had dropped half an octave. "We've three weeks. . . ." And for the first time in his life he looked forward to three undiluted weeks of one woman's company. It was like scenting one's mate, primordial and reflexive, and while his intellect ignored the peremptory, inexplicable compulsion, his body and blood and dragooned sensory receptors willingly complied to the urgency.

Bending his head low, his lips touched hers lightly, brushing twice across them like silken warmth before he gently slid over her mouth with his tongue and sent a shocking trail of fire curling deep down inside her.

She drew back in an unconscious response, but he'd felt the heated flame, too, and from the startled look in his eyes she knew the spark had touched them both. Trey's breathing quickened, his hand tightened abruptly on the back of her head, pulling her closer with insistence, with authority, while his other hand slid down her back until it rested warmly at the base of her spine. And when his mouth covered hers a second time, intense suddenly, more demanding, she could feel him rising hard against her. She may have been an innocent in the ways of a man and a woman, but Empress knew how animals mated in nature, and for the first time she sensed a soft warmth stirring within herself.

It was at once strange and blissful, and for a brief detached moment she felt very grown, as if a riddle of the universe were suddenly revealed. One doesn't have to love a man to feel the fire, she thought. It was at odds with all her mother had told her. Inexplicably she experienced an overwhelming sense of discovery, as if she alone knew a fundamental principle of humanity. But then her transient musing was abruptly arrested, for under the light pressure of Trey's lips she found hers opening, and the velvety, heated caress of Trey's tongue slowly entered her mouth, exploring languidly, licking her sweetness, and the heady, brandy taste of him was like a fresh treasure to be savored. She tentatively responded like a lambkin to new, unsteady legs, and when her tongue brushed his and did her own unhurried tasting, she heard him groan low in his throat. Swaying gently against her, his hard length pressed more adamantly into her yielding softness. Fire raced downward to a tingling place deep inside her as Trey's strong, insistent arousal throbbed against the soft curve of her stomach. He held her captive with his large hand low on her back as they kissed, and she felt a leaping flame speed along untried nerve endings, creating delicious new sensations. There was strange pleasure in the feel of his soft wool shirt; a melting warmth seeped through her senses, and she swayed closer into the strong male body, as if she knew instinctively that he would rarefy the enchantment. A moment later, as her mouth opened pliantly beneath his, her hands came up of their own accord and, rich with promise, rested lightly on his shoulders.

Her artless naïveté was setting his blood dangerously afire. He gave her high marks for subtlety. First the tentative withdrawal, and now the ingenuous response, was more erotic than any flagrant vice of the most skilled lover. And yet it surely must be some kind of drama, effective like the scene downstairs, where she withheld more than she offered in the concealing men's clothes and made every man in the room want to undress her.

Whether artifice, pretext, sham, or entreating supplication, the soft, imploring body melting into his, the small appealing hands warm on his shoulders, made delay suddenly inconvenient. "I think, sweet Empress," he said, his breath warm on her mouth, "*next* time you can set the pace. . . ."

Bending quickly, he lifted her into his arms and carried her to the bed. Laying her down on the rose velvet coverlet, he stood briefly and looked at her. Wanton as a Circe nymph, she looked back at him, her glance direct into his heated gaze, and she saw the smoldering, iridescent desire in his eyes. She was golden pearl juxtaposed to blush velvet, and when she slowly lifted her arms to him, he, no longer in control of himself, not detached or casual or playful as he usually was making love, took a deep breath, swiftly moved the half step to the bed, and lowered his body over hers, reaching for the buttons on his trousers with trembling fingers. His boots crushed the fine velvet but he didn't notice; she whimpered slightly when his heavy gold belt buckle pressed into her silken skin, but he kissed her in apology, intent on burying himself in the devastating Miss Jordan's lushly carnal body. His wool-clad legs pushed her pale thighs apart, and all he could think of was the feel of her closing around him. He surged forward, and she cried out softly. Maddened with desire, he thrust forward again. This time he *heard* her cry. "Oh, Christ," he breathed, urgent need suffocating in his lungs, "you can't be a virgin." He never bothered with virgins. It had been years since he'd slept with one. Lord, he was hard.

"It doesn't matter," she replied quickly, tense beneath him.

"It doesn't matter," he repeated softly, blood drumming in his temples and in his fingertips and in the soles of his feet inside the custom-made boots, and most of all in his rigid erection, insistent like a battering ram a hair's breadth from where he wanted to be so badly, he could taste the blood in his mouth. It doesn't matter, his conscience repeated. She said it doesn't matter, so it doesn't matter, and he drove in again.

Her muffled cry exploded across his lips as his mouth lowered to kiss her.

"Oh, hell." He exhaled deeply, drawing back, and, poised on his elbows, looked down at her uncertainly, his long dark hair framing his face like black silk.

"I won't cry out again," she whispered, her voice more certain than the poignant depths of her shadowy eyes. "Please . . . I must have the money."

It was all too odd and too sudden and too out of character for him. Damn . . . plundering a virgin, making her cry in fear and pain. *Steady, you'll live if you don't have her*, he told himself, but quivering need played devil's advocate to that platitude. She was urging him on. His body was even more fiercely demanding he take her. "Hell and damnation," he muttered disgruntedly. The problem was terrible, demanding immediate answers and he wasn't thinking too clearly, only feeling a delirious excitement quite detached from moral judgment. And adamant. "Bloody hell," he breathed, and in that moment, rational thought gained a fingertip control on the ragged edges of his lust. "Keep the money. I don't want to—" He said it quickly, before he'd change his mind, then paused and smiled. "Obviously that's not entirely true, but I don't ruin virgins," he said levelly.

Empress had not survived the death of her parents and the months following, struggling to stay alive in the wilderness, without discovering in herself immense strength. She summoned it now, shakily but determinedly. "It's not a moral dilemma. It's a business matter and my responsibility. I insist."

He laughed, his smile close and deliciously warm. "Here I'm refusing a woman insisting I take her virginity. I must be crazy."

"The world's crazy sometimes, I think," she replied softly, aware of the complex reasons prompting her conduct.

"Tonight, at least," he murmured, "it's more off track than usual." But even for a wild young man notorious as a womanizer, the offered innocence was too strangely bizarre. And maybe too businesslike for a man who found pleasure and delight in the act. It was not flattering to be a surrogate for a business matter. "Look," he said with an obvious effort, "thanks but no thanks. I'm not interested. But keep the money. I admire your courage." And rolling off her, he lay on his back and shouted, "*Flo!*"

"No!" Empress cried, and was on top of him before he drew his next breath, terrified he'd change his mind about the money, terrified he'd change his mind in the morning when his head was clear and he woke up in Flo's arms. Fifty thousand dollars was a huge sum of money to give away on a whim, or to lose to some misplaced moral scruple. She must convince him to stay with her, then at least she could earn the money. Or at least try.

Lying like silken enchantment on his lean, muscled body, she covered his face with kisses. Breathless, rushing kisses, a young girls's simple closemouthed kisses. Then, in a flush of boldness, driven by necessity, a tentative dancing lick of her small tongue slid down his straight nose, to his waiting mouth. When her tongue lightly caressed the arched curve of his upper lip, his hands came up and closed on her naked shoulders, and he drew the teasing tip into his mouth. He sucked on it gently, slowly, as if he envisioned a lifetime without interruptions, until the small, sun-kissed shoulders beneath his hands trembled in tiny quivers.

Strange, fluttering wing beats sped through her heating blood, and a curious languor caused Empress to twine her arms around Trey's strong neck. But her heart was beating hard like the Indian drums whose sound carried far up to their hidden valley in summer, for fear outweighed languor still. He mustn't go to Flo. Slipping her fingers through the black luster of his long hair, ruffled in loose waves on his neck, she brushed her mouth along his cheek. "Please," she whispered near his ear, visions of her hope to save her family dashed by his reluctance, "stay with me." It was a simple plea, simply put. It was perhaps her last chance. Her lips traced the perfect curve of his ears, and his hands tightened their grip in response. "Say it's all right. Say I can stay. . . ." She was murmuring rapidly in a flurry of words.

How should he answer the half-shy, quicksilver words? Why was she insisting? Why did the flattery of a woman wanting him matter?

Then she shifted a little so her leg slid between his, a sensual, instinctive movement, and the smooth velvet of his masculinity rose against her thigh. It was warm, it was hot, and like a child might explore a new sensation, she moved her leg lazily up its length.

Trey's mouth went dry, and he couldn't convince himself that refusal was important any longer. He groaned, thinking, there are some things in life without answers. His hand was trembling when he drew her mouth back to his.

A moment later, when Flo knocked and called out his name, Empress shouted, "Go away!" And when Flo repeated his name, Trey's voice carried clearly through the closed door. "I'll be down later."

He was rigid but tense and undecided, and Empress counted on the little she knew about masculine desire to accomplish what her logical explanation hadn't. Being French, she was well aware that *amour* could be heated and fraught with urgent emotion, but she was unsure exactly about the degree of urgency relative to desire.

But she knew what had happened moments before when she'd tasted his mouth and recalled how he'd responded to her yielding softness, so she practiced her limited expertise with a determined persistence. She must be sure she had the money. And if it would assure her family their future, her virginity was paltry stuff in the bargain.

"Now let's begin again," she whispered.

THE MAGNIFICENT ROGUE
by Iris Johansen

On Sale in August

From the glittering court of Queen Elizabeth to the barren island of Craighdu, THE MAGNIFICENT ROGUE is the spellbinding story of courageous love and unspeakable evil. The daring chieftain of a Scottish clan, Robert MacDarren knows no fear, and only the threat to a kinsman's life makes him bow to Queen Elizabeth's order that he wed Kathryn Ann Kentrye. He's aware of the dangerous secret in Kate's past, a secret that could destroy a great empire, but he doesn't expect the stirring of desire when he first lays eyes on the fragile beauty. Grateful to escape the tyranny of her guardian, Kate accepts the mesmerizing stranger as her husband. But even as they discover a passion greater than either has known, enemies are weaving their poisonous web around them, and soon Robert and Kate must risk their very lives to defy the ultimate treachery.

In the following scene, Robert and his cousin Gavin Gordon have come to Kate's home to claim her—and she flees.

She was being followed!

Sebastian?

Kate paused a moment on the trail and caught a glimpse of dark hair and the shimmer of the gold necklace about her pursuer's neck. Not Sebastian. Robert MacDarren.

The wild surge of disappointment she felt at the realization was completely unreasonable. He must have come at Sebastian's bidding, which meant her guardian had persuaded him to his way of thinking. Well, what had she expected? He was a stranger and Sebastian was a respected man of the cloth. There was no reason why he would be different from any of the others. How clever of Sebastian to send someone younger and stronger than himself to search her out, she thought bitterly.

She turned and began to run, her shoes sinking into the mud with every step. She glanced over her shoulder.

He was closer. He was not running, but his long legs covered the ground steadily, effortlessly, as his gaze studied the trail in front of him. He had evidently not seen her yet and was only following her tracks.

She was growing weaker. Her head felt peculiarly light and her breath was coming in painful gasps. She couldn't keep running.

And she couldn't surrender.

Which left only one solution to her dilemma. She sprinted several yards ahead and then darted into the underbrush at the side of the trail.

Hurry. She had to hurry. Her gaze frantically searched the underbrush. Ah, there was one.

She pounced on a heavy branch and then backtracked several yards and held it, waiting.

She must aim for the head. She had the strength for only one blow and it must drop him.

Her breath sounded heavily and terribly loud. She had to breathe more evenly or he would hear her.

He was almost upon her.

Her hands tightened on the branch.

He went past her, his expression intent as he studied the tracks.

She drew a deep breath, stepped out on the trail behind him, and swung the branch with all her strength.

He grunted in pain and then slowly crumpled to the ground.

She dropped the branch and ran past his body and darted down the trail again.

Something struck the back of her knees. She was falling!

She hit the ground so hard, the breath left her body. Blackness swirled around her.

When the darkness cleared, she realized she was on her back, her arms pinned on each side of her head. Robert MacDarren was astride her body.

She started to struggle.

"Lie still, dammit." His hands tightened cruelly on her arms. "I'm not—Ouch!"

She had turned her head and sunk her teeth into his wrist. She could taste the coppery flavor of blood in her mouth, but his grip didn't ease.

"Let me go!" How stupidly futile the words were when she knew he had no intention of releasing her.

She tried to butt her head against his chest, but she couldn't reach him.

"Really, Robert, can't you wait until the words are said for you to climb on top of her?" Gavin Gordon said from behind MacDarren.

"It's about time you got here," MacDarren said in a growl. "She's trying to kill me."

'Aye, for someone who couldn't lift her head, she's doing quite well. I saw her strike the blow." Gavin grinned. "But I was too far away to come to your rescue. Did she do any damage?"

"I'm going to have one hell of a headache."

Kate tried to knee him in the groin, but he quickly moved upward on her body.

"Your hand's bleeding," Gavin observed.

"She's taken a piece out of me. I can see why Landfield kept the ropes on her."

The ropes. Despair tore through her as she realized how completely Sebastian had won him to his way of thinking. The man would bind her and take her back to Sebastian. She couldn't fight against both MacDarren and Gordon and would use the last of her precious strength trying to do so. She would have to wait for a better opportunity to present itself. She stopped fighting and lay there staring defiantly at him.

"Very sensible," MacDarren said grimly. "I'm not in a very good temper at the moment. I don't think you want to make it worse."

"Get off me."

"And have you run away again?" MacDarren shook his head. "You've caused me enough trouble for one day. Give me your belt, Gavin."

Gavin took off his wide leather belt and handed it to MacDarren, who buckled the belt about her wrists and drew it tight.

"I'm not going back to the cottage," she said with the fierceness born of desperation. "I *can't* go back there."

He got off her and rose to his feet. "You'll go where I tell you to go, even if I have to drag—" He stopped in self-disgust as he realized what he had said. "Christ, I sound like that bastard." The anger suddenly left him as he looked at her lying there before him. "You're afraid of him?"

Fear was always with her when she thought of Sebastian, but she would not admit it. She sat up and repeated, "I can't go back."

He studied her for a moment. "All right, we won't go back. You'll never have to see him again."

She stared at him in disbelief.

He turned to Gavin. "We'll stay the night at that inn we passed at the edge of the village. Go back to the cottage and get her belongings and then saddle the horses. We'll meet you at the stable."

Gavin nodded and the next moment disappeared into the underbrush.

MacDarren glanced down at Kate. "I trust you don't object to that arrangement?"

She couldn't comprehend his words. "You're taking me away?"

"If you'd waited, instead of jumping out the window, I would have told you that two hours ago. That's why I came."

Then she thought she understood. "You're taking me to the lady?"

He shook his head. "It appears Her Majesty thinks it's time you wed."

Shock upon shock. "Wed?"

He said impatiently, "You say that as if you don't know what it means. You must have had instructions on the duties of wifehood."

"I know what it means." Slavery and suffocation and cruelty. From what she could judge from Sebastian and Martha's marriage, a wife's lot was little better than her own. True, he did not beat Martha, but the screams she heard from their bedroom while they mated had filled her with sick horror. But she had thought she would never have to worry about that kind of mistreatment. "I can never marry."

"Is that what the good vicar told you?" His lips tightened. "Well, it appears the queen disagrees."

Then it might come to pass. Even Sebastian obeyed the queen. The faintest hope began to spring within her. Even though marriage was only another form of slavery, perhaps the queen had chosen an easier master than Sebastian for her. "Who am I to marry?"

He smiled sardonically. "I have that honor."

Another shock and not a pleasant one. Easy was not a term anyone would use to describe this man. She blurted, "And you're not afraid?"

"Afraid of you? Not if I have someone to guard my back."

That wasn't what she meant, but of course he wouldn't be afraid. She doubted if he feared anything or anyone, and, besides, she wasn't what Sebastian said she was. He had said the words so often, she sometimes found herself believing him, and she was so tired now, she wasn't thinking clearly. The strength was seeping out of her with every passing second. "No, you shouldn't be afraid." She swayed. "Not Lilith . . ."

"More like a muddy gopher," he muttered as he reached out and steadied her. "We have to get to the stable. Can you walk, or shall I carry you?"

"I can walk." She dismissed the outlandish thought of marriage from her mind. She would ponder the implications of this change in her life later. There were more important matters to consider now. "But we have to get Caird."

"Caird? Who the devil is Caird?"

"My horse." She turned and started through the underbrush. "Before we go I have to fetch him. He's not far. . . ."

She could hear the brush shift and whisper as he followed her. "Your horse is in the forest?"

"I was hiding him from Sebastian. He was going to kill him. He wanted me to tell him where he was."

"And that was why he was dragging you?"

She ignored the question. "Sebastian said the forest beasts would devour him. He frightened me." She was staggering with exhaustion, but she couldn't give up now. "It's been such a while since I left him." She rounded a corner of a trail and breathed a sigh of relief as she caught sight of Caird calmly munching grass under the shelter of an oak tree. "No, he's fine."

"You think so?" MacDarren's skeptical gaze raked the piebald stallion from its swayback to its knobby knees. "I see nothing fine about him. How old is he?"

"Almost twenty." She reached the horse and tenderly began to stroke his muzzle. "But he's strong and very good-tempered."

"He won't do," MacDarren said flatly. "We'll have to get rid of him. He'd never get through the Highlands. We'll leave him with the innkeeper and I'll buy you another horse."

"I *won't* get rid of him," she said fiercely. "I can't just leave him. How would I know if they'd take good care of him? He goes with us."

"And I say he stays."

The words were spoken with such absolute resolution that they sent a jolt of terror through her. They reminded her of Sebastian's edicts, from which there was no appeal. She moistened her lips. "Then I'll have to stay too."

MacDarren's gaze narrowed on her face. "And what if Landfield catches you again?"

She shrugged and leaned her cheek wearily against Caird's muzzle. "He belongs to me," she said simply.

She could feel his gaze on her back and sensed his exasperation. "Oh, for God's sake!" He picked up her saddle from the ground by the tree and threw it on Caird's back. He began to buckle the cinches. "All right, we'll take him."

Joy soared through her. "Truly?"

"I said it, didn't I?" He picked her up and tossed her into the saddle. "We'll use him as a pack horse and I'll get you another mount to ride. Satisfied?"

Satisfied! She smiled brilliantly. "Oh yes. You won't regret it. But you needn't spend your money on another horse. Caird is really very strong. I'm sure he'll be able to—"

"I'm already regretting it." His tone was distinctly edgy as he began to lead the horse through the forest. "Even carrying a light load, I doubt if he'll get through the Highlands."

It was the second time he had mentioned these forbidding Highlands, but she didn't care where they were going as long as they were taking Caird. "But you'll do it? You won't change your mind?"

For an instant his expression softened as he saw the eagerness in her face. "I won't change my mind."

Gavin was already mounted and waiting when they arrived at the stable a short time later. A grin lit his face as he glanced from Kate to the horse and then back again. "Hers?"

Robert nodded. "And the cause of all this turmoil."

"A fitting pair," Gavin murmured. "She has a chance of cleaning up decently, but the horse . . ." He shook his head. "No hope for it, Robert."

"My thought exactly. But we're keeping him anyway."

Gavin's brows lifted. "Oh, are we? Interesting . . ."

Robert swung into the saddle. "Any trouble with the vicar and his wife?"

Kate's hands tensed on the reins.

"Mistress Landfield appeared to be overjoyed to give me the girl's belongings." He nodded at a small bundle tied to the saddle. "And the vicar just glowered at me."

"Perhaps he's given up."

"He won't give up," Kate whispered. "He never gives up."

"Then perhaps we'd better go before we encounter him again," Robert said as he kicked his horse into a trot. "Keep an eye on her, Gavin. She's almost reeling in that saddle."

Sebastian was waiting for them a short distance from the cottage. He stood blocking the middle of the path.

"Get out of the way," Robert said coldly. "I'm not in the mood for this."

"It's your last chance," Sebastian said. "Give her back to me before it's too late."

"Stand aside, Landfield."

"Kathryn." Sebastian turned to her and his voice was pleading. "Do not go. You know you can never wed. You know what will happen."

Robert rode forward and his horse's shoulder forced Sebastian to the side of the trail. He motioned Gavin and Kate to ride ahead. "It's over. She's no longer your responsibility." His voice lowered to soft deadliness. "And if you ever approach her again, I'll make sure I never see you repeat the mistake."

"You'll see me." Landfield's eyes shimmered with tears as his gaze clung to Kate. "I wanted to spare you, Kathryn. I wanted to save you, but God has willed otherwise. You know what has to be done now."

He turned and walked heavily back toward the cottage.

"What did he mean?" Gavin asked as his curious gaze followed Landfield.

She didn't answer as she watched Sebastian stalk away. She realized she was shivering with a sense of impending doom. How foolish. This was what he wanted her to feel, his way of chaining her to him.

"Well?" Robert asked.

"Nothing. He just wanted to make me afraid." She moistened her lips. "He likes me to be afraid of him."

She could see he didn't believe her and thought he would pursue it. Instead he said quietly, "You don't have to fear him any longer. He no longer holds any power over you." He held her gaze with a mesmerizing power. "I'm the only one who does now."

OFFICIAL RULES TO WINNERS CLASSIC SWEEPSTAKES

No Purchase necessary. To enter the sweepstakes follow instructions found elsewhere in this offer. You can also enter the sweepstakes by hand printing your name, address, city, state and zip code on a 3" x 5" piece of paper and mailing it to: Winners Classic Sweepstakes, P.O. Box 785, Gibbstown, NJ 08027. Mail each entry separately. Sweepstakes begins 12/1/91. Entries must be received by 6/1/93. Some presentations of this sweepstakes may feature a deadline for the Early Bird prize. If the offer you receive does, then to be eligible for the Early Bird prize your entry must be received according to the Early Bird date specified. Not responsible for lost, late, damaged, misdirected, illegible or postage due mail. Mechanically reproduced entries are not eligible. All entries become property of the sponsor and will not be returned.

Prize Selection/Validations: Winners will be selected in random drawings on or about 7/30/93, by VENTURA ASSOCIATES, INC., an independent judging organization whose decisions are final. Odds of winning are determined by total number of entries received. Circulation of this sweepstakes is estimated not to exceed 200 million. Entrants need not be present to win. All prizes are guaranteed to be awarded and delivered to winners Winners will be notified by mail and may be required to complete an affidavit of eligibility and release of liability which must be returned within 14 days of date of notification or alternate winners will be selected. Any guest of a trip winner will also be required to execute a release of liability. Any prize notification letter or any prize returned to a participating sponsor, Bantam Doubleday Dell Publishing Group, Inc., its participating divisions or subsidiaries, or VENTURA ASSOCIATES, INC. as undeliverable will be awarded to an alternate winner. Prizes are not transferable. No multiple prize winners except as may be necessary due to unavailability, in which case a prize of equal or greater value will be awarded. Prizes will be awarded approximately 90 days after the drawing. All taxes, automobile license and registration fees, if applicable, are the sole responsibility of the winners. Entry constitutes permission (except where prohibited) to use winners' names and likenesses for publicity purposes without further or other compensation.

Participation: This sweepstakes is open to residents of the United States and Canada, except for the province of Quebec. This sweepstakes is sponsored by Bantam Doubleday Dell Publishing Group, Inc. (BDD), 666 Fifth Avenue, New York, NY 10103. Versions of this sweepstakes with different graphics will be offered in conjunction with various solicitations or promotions by different subsidiaries and divisions of BDD. Employees and their families of BDD, its division, subsidiaries, advertising agencies, and VENTURA ASSOCIATES, INC., are not eligible.

Canadian residents, in order to win, must first correctly answer a time limited arithmetical skill testing question. Void in Quebec and wherever prohibited or restricted by law. Subject to all federal, state, local and provincial laws and regulations.

Prizes: The following values for prizes are determined by the manufacturers' suggested retail prices or by what these items are currently known to be selling for at the time this offer was published. Approximate retail values include handling and delivery of prizes. Estimated maximum retail value of prizes: 1 Grand Prize ($27,500 if merchandise or $25,000 Cash); 1 First Prize ($3,000); 5 Second Prizes ($400 each); 35 Third Prizes ($100 each); 1,000 Fourth Prizes ($9.00 each); 1 Early Bird Prize ($5,000); Total approximate maximum retail value is $50,000. Winners will have the option of selecting any prize offered at level won. Automobile winner must have a valid driver's license at the time the car is awarded. Trips are subject to space and departure availability. Certain black-out dates may apply. Travel must be completed within one year from the time the prize is awarded. Minors must be accompanied by an adult. Prizes won by minors will be awarded in the name of parent or legal guardian.

For a list of Major Prize Winners (available after 7/30/93): send a self-addressed, stamped envelope entirely separate from your entry to: Winners Classic Sweepstakes Winners, P.O. Box 825, Gibbstown, NJ 08027. Requests must be received by 6/1/93. DO NOT SEND ANY OTHER CORRESPONDENCE TO THIS P.O. BOX.

Don't miss these fabulous Bantam women's fiction titles on sale in May